Range Boss

Range Boss Jack Carlsen has a fight on his hands. The Bar Circle spread, once prosperous, is now on the verge of going bust. The owner has been found dead in a whore's bed, leaving behind debt and unhappy ranch-hands who talk of quitting. The Bar Circle's cattle have been taken by rustlers and the new owner is struggling to defend the ranch. Hearing of the ranch's plight and spying the chance to make a quick profit, men are circling like coyotes, ready to kill anyone who stands in their way.

Carlsen vowed he'd finished with gunfighting ten years ago. But how can the Bar Circle survive without his help? He knows he must buckle on his gunbelt once again.

Range Boss

Jack Edwardes

A Black Horse Western

ROBERT HALE · LONDON

© Jack Edwardes 2015
First published in Great Britain 2015

ISBN 978-0-7198-1651-2

Robert Hale Limited
Clerkenwell House
Clerkenwell Green
London EC1R 0HT

www.halebooks.com

Typeset by
Derek Doyle & Associates, Shaw Heath
Printed and bound in Great Britain by
CPI Antony Rowe, Chippenham and Eastbourne

CHAPTER ONE

Jack Carlsen was stamping out the fire which he'd needed during the cool night of early summer when he heard the shots. He didn't give them much thought, probably someone out hunting for his breakfast. But then he heard the distinct thump of a scatter-gun, closely followed by several shots from a sidearm.

He glanced at the ashes to confirm they were dead and strode quickly to his palomino which he'd saddled earlier. He swung up to his saddle, and touched his heels to the sides of the animal, ducking low as he cleared the stand of cottonwoods.

On the trail below him, maybe two or three hundred yards away, a buggy was bowling along the trail to Jensen Flats. A heavy-shouldered man, wearing a city suit and a grey Stetson, held the buggy reins, urging on a grey pony. Alongside him, balancing himself against the sway of the buggy stood a younger man, a scatter-gun raised. He was aiming at the masked rider, who was firing a handgun held above the head of a ewe-necked horse which seemed unable to close the gap.

As Carlsen watched, the younger man fired the scatter-gun once more, and above the rattle of the spinning wheels of the buggy, Carlsen heard a cry of pain as the pursuer was hit. There was a shout of triumph from the men in the buggy as the bandit swerved away, heading for the higher ground. The buggy drew level with Carlsen, although neither driver nor passenger gave any indication they had seen him observing the chase.

'Well, I'm damned,' Carlsen muttered aloud as he recognized the occupants of the buggy. 'What the heck's goin' on here?'

He pulled his Winchester from its scabbard and turned the head of his palomino. If he was quick he could cut off the bandit who appeared to know the ground. Carlsen guessed he meant to seek cover in the trees before making his escape to the east. There was no sign of a long gun on the bandit's horse. Maybe the attempt at a hold-up was an act of desperation by some saddle-tramp.

'There's one way to find out,' he said aloud.

Three minutes of hard riding took him to the cottonwoods where the bandit had taken shelter. His Winchester at the ready, Carlsen walked his horse along the outermost ring of trees, alert to the danger of the bandit breaking through behind him. He'd made maybe fifty yards when he heard a horse snicker.

'I've got a long gun on you,' Carlsen shouted. 'C'mon out, an' no tricks!'

There was a pause and then the sound of branches being pushed aside reached him from somewhere ahead.

'If I shoot, I'm gonna kill you,' Carlsen shouted, still unsure exactly where the bandit was hiding.

'Don't shoot! Please don't shoot!'

The voice was muffled by the trees but Carlsen heard the appeal clearly, and he relaxed. This was no desperate hold-up or vicious saddle-tramp he'd cornered but he kept his long gun at the ready. There was nothing to gain by taking too many chances.

'C'mon out. You reach for a gun an' you're dead!'

He waited a few moments and was about to call out again when a few yards ahead, a horse broke through the ring of trees. A young boy, dressed only in ragged blue strap-coveralls and a battered brown hat, his bandanna now pulled from his face, ducked low over the pommel of his saddle to avoid the lower branches of the trees. A spattering of blood marked his shoulder. Carlsen watched as the boy cleared the trees and turned his mount's head.

'What's your name, boy?'

'Name's . . .' the boy muttered. His head was down and his words were lost.

'Speak up! I asked you your name.'

The boy raised his head. 'Ethan Ford,' he said clearly.

'An' how old are you?'

'I'm fourteen.' The boy's expression became defiant. 'But I'll be fifteen in a few weeks if Ma got the day right.'

'What in tarnation were you tryin' back there?'

'Tryin' to get the money stolen from my pa.'

'You know who was in that buggy?'

'Walter Hendrix an' his son, Grant.'

'An' why d' ya reckon the owners of the biggest ranch in these parts should steal from your pa?'

'Cos Grant Hendrix and three men told Pa to get off his land or they'd be back to kill the whole family.'

Carlsen suddenly recognized the boy. 'Is Daley Ford your pa?'

'Yes, sir.'

'What d'you think he's gonna say when I tell him what you've been doin'?'

'Pa ain't hereabouts anymore. Him an' all my kinfolk left a week ago. Pa said it weren't no use anymore tryin' to make a go of things here an' he was joinin' a wagon train headin' west.'

'So how come you're still hereabouts?'

'There's a coupla loose timbers at the back o' the shanty. Pa never did get to fixin' 'em. When Hendrix an' his men arrived I loosed them, crawled out and then hid among the cottonwoods.' The boy looked defiantly at Carlsen. 'That sonovabitch Hendrix ain't gonna chase me away.'

'Don't cuss, Ethan, you ain't old enough.'

Carlsen eased back on his reins as his palomino skittered a few feet across the bunch and buffalo grass. This was turning into a real barrel of tar. He'd thought when he headed back to the Bar Circle, he'd gotten ready for the arrival of the new owner but Ethan Ford was a problem he hadn't expected. If Ethan had been older and vicious he'd have taken him into the sheriff, but a boy trying to stand up for himself, even if he had acted foolishly, deserved something better. Anyway, the boy was right. Walter Hendrix was a son of a bitch.

'You still livin' in that sod shanty your kinfolk had?'

Ethan shook his head. 'Hendrix's men took it over to store their gear when they were rebranding our cattle.'

'OK, I'm gonna take you to the Bar Circle. I'll find you work there, an' we'll fix your shoulder. You gotta promise no more fancy tricks like the one today. We gotta deal?'

Ethan nodded. 'It's a deal, Mr Carlsen.'

'You know who I am?'

Ethan nodded and turned his mount's head. 'Hope you don't go fast. My old horse ain't up to it.'

Carlsen sat easily in the saddle of the big palomino. If his silver timepiece was correct and the 10.15 was on time, he'd soon be seeing the UP locomotive. Unlike his father who'd hated the railroad almost as much as the Shoshone, he'd been fascinated by these iron monsters since Jensen Flats got its spur line back in '68.

When times at the ranch were really bad, he'd even thought of taking the railroad to Cheyenne and then east to New York or maybe west to San Francisco. He'd wear a city suit and a derby hat, go to work in a city store, or maybe look after horses for a wealthy family who would tell their friends they'd hired 'a real cowboy'. Maybe he'd save enough money to buy a little house. Hell, he might even get married again.

Then he'd look out of the window of his room across the Territory of Wyoming towards the Big Horns and know that given the chance, he'd live and work on the ranch for the rest of his life, and yes, hope to die there. The Bar Circle had sent him down a different path in his life and that was good enough for him. For the last ten years he'd worked to keep the ranch together, honouring the memory of Jackson Nicholls who'd hired him when others wouldn't give him the time of day, scared of his reputation.

Even during the last three years with James Nicholls as the owner, he hadn't wavered. Nicholls's drinking and whoring, his high-spending, and his gambling had almost ruined the ranch but now there was a chance to start again with a new owner. Not a lot was known of JB Nicholls but he was said to be keen on restoring the ranch's fortunes.

The whistle of the train cut into Carlsen's thinking and half a mile down the track, the UP engine rounded the bend and began to slow as it approached the railroad stop. Carlsen looked around for the Bar Circle wagon. Fred Baker, the wagon driver, waved an acknowledgement of Carlsen's raised hand, and with a flick of the reins, Baker prompted the mule to turn the wagon and make for where the car carrying passengers' boxes would stop.

Carlsen got down from his saddle and climbed the wooden steps to stand alongside the scattering of townsfolk waiting to board the train. Towering above Carlsen's six feet

9

two, the UP loco, emitting a final blast of steam, drew slowly past him, and with a screeching of metal came to a halt. Carlsen stood several yards from where the best railcars were stopped, watching the conductor open the door and settle the flight of steps.

The town's lawyer, William Kurtz, stepped down to the ground. He wore a dark grey suit of fine material and a brushed grey derby. The cost of his clothes, Carlsen reckoned, would have been more than his own pay for a month. The lawyer walked towards him as Kurtz's buggy arrived, driven by his clerk.

'Good day, Jack. I'd have thought you'd be with the beef.' Kurtz greeted him with a raised hand.

For a moment, Carlsen remained expressionless. Kurtz may have met the new owner of the Bar Circle on the journey from Cheyenne. There'd be plenty of work for a lawyer if the new owner decided to sell. Had Kurtz put the notion of selling in the mind of the new owner? But maybe he was being harsh. Kurtz wasn't a bad fellow.

'New owner arrives today, Mr Kurtz.'

'Ah, yes.'

He smiled as if he knew something Carlsen didn't. 'I guess we'll be seeing each other in The Meadow once the beef are settled.'

Without waiting for Carlsen to reply, the lawyer headed for his buggy. A few moments later while Carlsen was thinking about Kurtz, a figure stepped down from the railcar, handing the conductor something which caused the conductor to smile and tug at the front of his cap.

Carlsen closed his eyes for a moment. Maybe when he opened them again the figure would be dressed differently. He took another look but nothing had changed. The man's pure white Stetson sported an extra-wide brim adorned with nickel spangles around the band. His white shirt with a broad turndown collar was set off by a flowing blue tie. Around his waist, the shiny new cartridge belt fitted snugly above his corduroy riding breeches and glistening boots. To complete the picture, he wore nickel spurs with large Californian rowels.

Carlsen breathed in deeply. He remembered an old Spanish proverb. 'Be careful what you wish for.' He'd wanted a new owner for a long time, and now he'd got one. He'd better make the best of it. He walked over to greet the newcomer who was peering around, looking lost.

'Howdy, Mr Nicholls, the name's Carlsen, range boss of the Bar Circle.'

The man looked at him, surprise registering on his smooth pale face. 'JB's still on the train, Carlsen. I'm Hector Davis, JB's business manager.' He thrust out his hand. 'Thank you for meeting us.'

Despite his crazy get-up, Carlsen decided, Davis was an amiable man. But business manager? What the hell was that?

'One of the hands has a wagon for all your boxes, Mr Davis.' Carlsen half-turned and pointed. 'He's loading them now.'

'Then I'd better check that he has the right ones.' Davis glanced down, a puzzled expression on his face. 'You're not wearing a gun, Carlsen. I thought you cowboys always carried a gun.'

Carlsen grinned. 'Only in Ned Buntline stories, Mr Davis. Jensen's a peaceful town. I don't see the need to carry a gun when I'm meeting my new boss.'

'No, I guess not. You'll not leave without me?' Davis added anxiously.

'The surrey will be here in a coupla minutes.'

Carlsen stood back to watch Davis hurry away to the end of the train where Baker and a railroad employee were

11

loading boxes on to the wagon. He turned back to see a young woman step down from the train, assisted by the conductor who wished her a comfortable stay. Carlsen liked her smile as she thanked the conductor for his good wishes. She wore a blue silk dress, and over her shoulders was a fancy coloured shawl. Her fair hair was partly covered with a blue hat, its veil folded back. In one hand she held an opened parasol. Although Carlsen knew nothing about women's stuff he could see that her clothes had cost money. The older woman behind her, Carlsen guessed, was the maid of the young woman.

The young woman was probably a guest of the English Lord Frewen whose ranch was some distance from Jensen. Carlsen guessed a smart carriage would be along soon as she was obviously expecting to be met. He looked in the direction of the town but no carriage was heading their way. On an impulse, he stepped forward, his forefinger briefly touching the brim of his hat.

'Howdy, ma'am. Can I be of some assistance?'

'Thank you,' she said. 'I'm expecting someone from the Bar Circle ranch to meet me.'

Carlsen frowned. 'I'm from the Bar Circle, ma'am. The name's Carlsen, but I'm here to meet the new owner.'

'JB Nicholls?'

'That's right, ma'am.'

The young woman's eyes gleamed. 'I am JB Nicholls. James Nicholls was my uncle.' She turned the handle of her parasol in her hand. 'Are you one of the ranch hands?'

'You could say that. I'm the range boss.'

'And what does that mean?'

Carlsen was silent for a moment. He wasn't used to questions being thrown at him by anyone, let alone by a young woman who looked as if she'd stepped out of one of those fancy magazines from back east he'd seen around the

General Store. He didn't like it, even if the questioner was as pretty as a flower in spring. He looked directly at her and became aware she was waiting for him to reply, looking straight into his eyes.

'I answer for everything that happens on the ranch,' he said. 'I take charge of the spring and fall round-ups, seein' the cattle are bred up, makin' sure they get the water they need, checkin' the irrigation ditches are dug or extended, keepin' the corrals in good repair, makin' sure the men are doin' the job they're bein' paid for.'

She nodded, apparently satisfied, and looked around. 'How far is the ranch and how do we get there?'

Over her shoulder, Carlsen saw the surrey approaching. Sean had obviously fixed the broken wheel which had delayed his arrival.

'Coupla hours, ma'am, the surrey is arriving now for you and Mr Davis.' He looked around. 'I guess him and Baker are finishin' up right now.'

As he spoke, he saw Davis hand something to the railroad worker who touched his hat in response. Maybe a business manager just went around giving folks money. The surrey, pulled by a big roan, drew up alongside Carlsen as, with a final word to Baker, Davis began to retrace his steps towards them, the morning sun glinting on the metal of his Stetson band.

'I assume you're riding back to the ranch, Mr Carlsen.'

'Yes, ma'am. My palomino's back o' the station house.'

'Good. I may wish to stop the carriage and ask more questions.'

Carlsen was aware that Sean shot him a glance as the ranch-hand jumped smartly to the ground, extending a hand to assist the new owner to step into the surrey. She's going to have everyone running around like prairie-dogs, Carlsen thought, as he became aware of Davis's hurried steps behind him.

'Back to the ranch, Sean,' he ordered. 'I'll get my horse, an' be with you.'

Two hours later, the surrey rolled beneath the swinging wooden sign that marked the land around the Big House of the Bar Circle spread. Carlsen was riding alongside the surrey. They'd made a speedy journey from Jensen. His new boss had stopped Sean only twice. Once when they'd passed The Meadow and Carlsen had explained that it was used by the men to practice for the annual shooting contest, and then when she'd spotted a group of half a dozen riders crossing the trail ahead of them.

'Indians, Mr Carlsen. Are they likely to attack us?' she'd asked.

For a young white woman to ask such a question she appeared remarkably calm, Carlsen had thought.

'No, ma'am,' he'd replied. 'They're Shoshone and friendly with us white folks.'

She'd nodded, and tapped Sean's shoulder with her folded parasol. 'Carry on, please.'

Another mile and the buildings of the Bar Circle came into view. Shortly after, Sean halted the roan in front of the ranch-house and jumped to the ground as Carlsen swung down from his saddle. JB Nicholls took Sean's outstretched hand and stepped down to the ground. Behind her, the maid and Davis alighted from the other side of the surrey.

The new owner stood looking around her. The ranch-house was a big two-storey structure built of heavy timber, with a porch which ran around to the rear and stout timbers at each corner set on a foundation of stone. It was a fine building but there were signs that it needed some money spent on its maintenance.

'I'll show you the place tomorrow, ma'am,' Carlsen said, pointing across to the cluster of buildings surrounding the

14

ranch-house. 'If Mr Davis tells Sean the boxes you all need tonight, he'll have them placed in your rooms.' He looked towards the high door of the ranch house, in front of which stood a plump woman of about forty and a young girl. 'Mrs Gittins is your housekeeper and the cook, Lucy, helps around the house. She'll show you your rooms, and the room for your maid.'

'Thank you, Mr Carlsen. I'm tired now, and I shall rest. I assume you'll be ready for an early start tomorrow. I wish to ride out and see the men and the cattle.'

'Mebbe we can talk about it over supper, ma'am.'

She was silent for a few seconds. Then she turned to Davis. 'Hector,' she said, and turned on her heel to approach the two women waiting at the door.

Davis waited until the four women had entered the house. 'Don't take offence, Carlsen,' he said. 'I guess we're not familiar with your ways out here in the west. JB's not used to having hired hands sharing her table. The only people she allows to remain in the house are the house servants and they eat in the kitchen.'

Carlsen grunted. 'I've had a room in this house since old Jackson Nicholls got sick in his last year.' He shrugged. 'But if that's the way, JB—' He stopped and grimaced. 'I ain't gonna call her that. I don't see no rings on her hands so I guess she's not married.'

'That's correct.'

'An' what does the J stand for?'

'Jane.'

'Then you'd better tell her she's gonna be "Miss Jane" around the Bar Circle.'

Davis smiled. 'OK, Carlsen, I'll tell her.'

'An' as you're givin' orders, tell Sean I want all the stuff from my room shifted to the shanty afore he gets his supper.'

'I'll do that.'

Carlsen looked hard at Davis. 'After Mr Jackson died we had trouble for too many years with his son. I hope we ain't gonna have trouble with Miss Jane.'

Carlsen turned on his heel and headed for the shanty.

CHAPTER TWO

Carlsen had been up and around, checking on the corral fences for a couple of hours. He'd just decided to have a couple of men carry out repair work when Sean came to tell him that Miss Jane was ready to ride out.

'You got Ethan workin'?' Carlsen asked.

'Cleanin' all the saddles. He's doin' a good job.'

'OK, I'll get my mount,' Carlsen said. 'Bring out the grulla, he's a quiet ride.' He grinned. 'He might even show Miss Jane a coupla tricks.'

'Miss Jane tol' me she wants the Appaloosa. She had a look at him last night.'

Carlsen frowned. 'When was that?'

'I reckon when you was havin' supper.'

Carlsen shrugged. 'OK, she's the boss.'

He walked across to the barn where he found Ethan leading the palomino towards him.

'Mornin', Mr Carlsen. I gave your saddle a clean.'

'Looks good, Ethan. Sean tol' me you're doin' a fine job.'

Ethan's face split in a big grin. 'Tryin' to, Mr Carlsen.'

Carlsen looked up and down at the boy who still wore his old coveralls, now covering a patched red undershirt. 'You goin' into town today?'

Ethan nodded. 'Me an' Sean haveta pick up some stuff for the horses.'

Carlsen thrust a hand in his pants pocket and pulled out a few coins. 'You get yourself new boots, a pair of Levis an' a coupla workin' shirts. First, you get to the bathhouse an' clean up.' He looked across at Sean. 'When you get back from town, you get some scissors from Mrs Gittins an' cut his hair.'

'Sure thing, boss.'

Ethan stared down at the coins handed to him by Carlsen. 'Jeepers, Mr Carlsen! It's gonna take some time to pay you back.'

'Then don't quit Wyoming,' Carlsen said dryly. He turned to Sean who'd been watching the pair with an amused expression on his face. 'C'mon, Sean, we'll see how Miss Jane takes to ridin'.'

Half an hour later, he was standing beside his palomino alongside Sean who held the Appaloosa. The animal could be skittish and an accident during Jane Nicholls's first ride would not be a good beginning. The door of the ranch house opened, and Jane Nicholls crossed the porch and stepped down to the hardpack in front of the house.

She wore a soft hat, a riding habit with a dark green skirt, and her jacket with its low collar showed a flowing red tie. Her boots, reaching to the hem of the skirt, gleamed. In her hand she held a short leather whip. She might have a tongue like a rattler, Carlsen thought, but she was still the prettiest woman he'd ever seen.

'Morning, Miss Jane.'

She looked at him sharply, not returning his greeting. Instead she tapped the saddle of the Appaloosa Sean was holding. 'What is this?'

'That's a saddle, ma'am,' Carlsen said, poker-faced. 'You haveta sit—'

'You're being impertinent, Mr Carlsen,' she snapped. 'Do you not have a side-saddle?'

If you were not the owner of this ranch, Carlsen thought, I'd damn well put you across my knee. Instead, he kept his voice even. If the Bar Circle was to survive he needed to be on good terms with JB Nicholls.

'Your grandmother always rode side-saddle, Miss Jane. I guess we have the saddle somewhere.'

'Boss, I reckon I know where it might be,' Sean said quickly. He looped the reins of the Appaloosa over the pommel of Carlsen's palomino. 'I'll be real quick,' he promised and scampered away.

'You obviously remember my grandmother,' Jane Nicholls said.

'Yes, ma'am. I was workin' here for five years afore the cholera took 'em.'

'Was it a surprise when my uncle took over?'

'I knew Mr Jackson's other two sons were killed in the War. But yeah, it was somethin' of a surprise. I don't think Mr James was cut out for ranchin'.'

'So I've been told.'

She broke off as Sean came running across, carrying the side-saddle in his arms.

'It's been cleaned every week with the other saddles, an' I've dusted it down,' he said breathlessly.

'That was quick, Sean. Thank you.'

If Sean had been a puppy dog, Carlsen reckoned, Sean would have been rolling on his back, feet in the air, waiting for his belly to be scratched. Carlsen hoped she didn't expect the same from him. But then he checked himself. There was nothing to gain by being ornery. He had a job to do and he'd better get on with it. He pointed out the various buildings around the house while Sean was changing the saddles.

19

'Bunkhouse and mess-house over to your right. All the men are up with the beef so the mess-house is empty. Beyond the bunkhouse is the blacksmith's shop. The big corral for the remuda is a ways beyond the corral for our own horses. That small corral is for the mule. Don't go near the brute. Sean's the only hand he'll let come close.'

'But the mule was pulling the wagon yesterday.'

'He's fine once he's between the shafts, ma'am. It's gettin' him there that's the problem,' Sean said as he tightened a cinch.

'We have a few chickens and pigs beyond the mule's corral,' Carlsen continued. 'An' a wired-in patch with two or three milkers for the house.'

'Give me an honest answer,' she said briskly. 'Is it all in good condition?'

Carlsen twisted his mouth for a second. 'It's like the Big House, ma'am, it's OK, but if we don't spend money soon we'll be in trouble.'

'Or we could sell out. I'm told there's a Walter Hendrix interested in buying.'

Carlsen's expression didn't change. 'I've heard that,' he said. 'He made your uncle an offer but he's backed off a while.'

She rapped her whip against her skirt. 'I'd better see the men and the stock. How long is the ride?'

'Coupla hours, I guess. We've finished the spring round-up an' we're movin' the beef for the summer. I've left a good man in charge.'

Jane Nicholls nodded, and moved around to the Appaloosa held by Sean. He put out his hand to assist her but this time she ignored his offer and stepped up lightly to the saddle, shifting until she was settled. Carlsen and Sean exchanged glances. Fancy lady from the east or not, Miss Jane Nicholls looked at ease on a horse.

Carlsen swung up to his saddle. 'Sean, no more than five hours, I guess. You got your work for today?'

'I'm gonna fix the boxes for Miss Jane, an' the rest. Mr Davis is gonna tell me what he wants. Then me an' Ethan are goin' into town.'

'Fine, keep Ethan at it, an' don't forget the scissors.'

'Sure, boss.'

Carlsen turned the head of the palomino, Jane Nicholls alongside him, and together they walked their mounts until they were clear of the ranch-house and the surrounding buildings. Carlsen touched his heels to the sides of his horse and the animal broke into a trot. Jane Nicholls did likewise and together, they headed for the higher ground where the cattle would spend the summer being fattened on the lush grass.

'Did my grandmother ride out often?' Jane Nicholls asked, as the horses trotted along, only a few feet apart.

'No, ma'am. She'd sometimes ride into town, and to see a neighbour. She used to take food to the nester's family durin' the end o' fall. Winters out here can be tough.'

Jane Nicholls looked puzzled. 'What does a nester do?'

'It's just a word, ma'am. A nester grabs a piece of open range and makes a home on it. Brings in a few cattle when he's built a cabin.'

'Is that lawful?'

'The law don't seem to be clear about that, providin' the nester goes for open range. If he don't try to grab too much land he don't worry anyone. But anyways, the one nester we had hereabouts quit a coupla weeks back, an' the Lazy Y folks have put stock on what they had.'

'Did my grandmother ever go out with the cattle?'

'No, ma'am. She reckoned that was a man's business.'

She looked directly at him. 'Supposing I said that I wished to ride out with the men?'

21

'Cowboys around cattle is no place for a lady, ma'am.'

Carlsen heard her blow out air in irritation. 'I'm the owner, Mr Carlsen. If I wish to ride out with the men I shall.'

Carlsen stared ahead. If he reined in, lifted Jane Nicholls from the saddle and put her across his knee, he'd be riding into Jensen in a couple of hours looking for a new job or planning to catch the UP loco east or west. And that, he decided, would be plumb crazy.

'If you're gonna do that, ma'am, you'll haveta change that saddle.'

Her head snapped around to glare at him but before he could say anything, she kicked her horse forward and within twenty yards, had urged the animal into a gallop, leaving Carlsen reined in, leaning on his pommel, and cursing under his breath.

They heard the cattle from some distance away. A dust cloud wafted in the blue sky above the animals as they slowly moved across the open land, heading for the richer grass. A dozen riders could be seen spread evenly on both sides of the mass of cattle. At the rear of the animals, a few hundred yards behind the two cowboys riding drag, a wagon stood stationary near a group of half a dozen cowboys. The men climbed to their feet, tin mugs in hand as Carlsen and Jane approached them.

'Howdy, boss. Howdy, ma'am,' called one of the cowboys, as the others joined in the greeting. The men exchanged puzzled looks, obviously wondering why a woman was riding with the range boss.

Carlsen swung down from his saddle, and held out his hand to assist Jane in dismounting. A little to his surprise, she took his hand, stepping lightly down to the grass.

'Everythin's fine, Mr Carlsen,' said a tall cowboy. 'Now we got 'em movin' Pete reckons we'll be settlin' 'em in a coupla days or so.'

'Heck! I'm gonna be outta job.' Carlsen grinned. He turned to Jane Nicholls. 'Pete Maxton's my top hand,' he explained. He gestured to the tall cowboy who had spoken. 'Blackie's next in line. Boys, meet the new owner of the Bar Circle, JB Nicholls. You'll address her with your best manners as Miss Jane. She's from the east but she can ride real well, an' she's talkin' about ridin' out with you sometime this summer.'

Carlsen grinned as a loud cheer went up, and Jane Nicholls held up a gloved hand in acknowledgement.

'OK,' Carlsen said. 'I just need to show Miss Jane a few things. Blackie, show Miss Jane a brandin' iron.'

Blackie reached into the wagon and pulled out a branding iron, holding it so Jane could examine the metal.

'A circle with a bar inside,' he explained. 'The first initial of the owner above and the second below the bar.' Blackie grinned. 'Good you've got the same initials, Miss Jane, or we'd be ridin' to Cheyenne to register a new brand.'

'All our cattle have this brand?'

'Yes, ma'am. That's what we've been about, makin' sure they get branded so if they get among the cattle from another ranch, we can find what belongs to us.'

'And did the work go well?'

Blackie hesitated, appearing to be reluctant to answer the question directly.

'Well, it's like this, ma'am—'

Jane's mouth set. 'Blackie, I'm not some girl from the east with her hair still down. I asked you a question and I expect an answer.'

'Rustlers have run off some of our cattle,' Carlsen cut in, seeing Blackie's face stiffen. 'We'll not know just how many until we get the beef settled agin.'

'Have you told the sheriff?'

23

'The sheriff will pay no mind, Miss Jane,' Blackie said. 'Mr Fenner looks after the town. He's not bothered by rustlers.'

She turned to Carlsen. 'Is the sheriff dishonest?'

'Fenner's straight as a ramrod. Out here we take care of our own business.'

She looked at him for a moment, and then nodded before turning away to remount her horse. In the saddle she looked down at Blackie.

'You're doing a fine job, Blackie. I hope before the summer is out you'll allow me to ride out with you to see the beef.'

Blackie appeared to grow another six inches, a beaming smile on his face, his earlier discomfort forgotten. 'Sure, Miss Jane. We're gonna look forward to that.' He half-turned. 'Ain't we, boys?'

A cheer went up from the group of cowboys, which was met with a smile from Jane as she turned the head of her horse. Carlsen turned his mount's head to follow her. He'd learned something during the ride. Miss Jane Nicholls was a whole heap smarter than he'd thought.

They were halfway back to the Bar Circle, both occupied with their thoughts, when Jane broke the silence between them. She brought her horse closer to Carlsen's palomino as their horses trotted along.

'Are you going to tell me more about someone stealing our cattle?'

For a moment, Carlsen almost wished that James Nicholls was still alive and kicking instead of cashing in his chips in a whore's bed. At least that member of the Nicholls family didn't hassle the range boss.

'We've lost about fifty head since the last count.'

'Could the men have made a mistake? It must be difficult to keep a check when the animals are moving around.'

24

'No, ma'am, the count's OK. We figure on losin' a few after the winter but the number's too high. Some no-good's been rustlin' our beef.'

'You sound very sure. What do you plan to do?'

'I'm gonna have to study on it.'

'We really must tell the sheriff in Jensen.'

Carlsen shook his head. 'Blackie was right, Miss Jane. Fenner will do nothin'. The circuit judge will say it's too difficult. The law in these parts leaves rustlers to the ranchers.'

'So what do you when you catch them?'

'We hang 'em, Miss Jane.'

There was a sharp intake of breath from Jane but she said nothing and for the remainder of the ride back to the Big House, she seemed content with her thoughts.

Sean and Ethan met them both at the house and took their horses, leading them away to the barn. Carlsen was pleased to see they hadn't wasted their wagon ride into town. Against the wall of the barn were stacked sacks of feed for the animals, ready for stowing in a water-tight store. Ethan was well-turned out in new Levis, a good pair of boots, and a blue shirt. His crop of thick hair was much neater.

Carlsen put a forefinger to his hat. 'I'll be gone for a while, ma'am. Pete Maxton's a good man but I'd be more easy if I was with the beef.'

'If Maxton is a good man I'd prefer you to remain here for a few days.'

Carlsen opened his mouth and then shut it firmly for a few seconds. It was true that he could rely on Maxton. 'OK, ma'am. If that's what you want. But there's only so much I can do around here.'

'Then you can start by riding into town and reporting the rustlers to Sheriff Fenner.'

'Ma'am, I tol' you earlier. It's not gonna help.'

'I know what you told me. You would hang any rustler you caught.' Her mouth set. 'We're not living in pioneer days. Wyoming will be a State one day, and the law should be enforced. The sheriff needs to be told.'

'That's good thinkin' out east, Miss Jane. You run by rules and lawmen to enforce them. Out here in the west, we haveta make up the rules as we go.'

'I wish you to report the rustlers to the sheriff, Mr Carlsen,' she said sharply. 'I think I'm making myself clear.'

'If that's what you want, ma'am,' he said. He turned away to avoid her looking at him. 'I'll be back early tomorrow.'

A couple of hours later, after grabbing coffee from Mrs Gittins at the Big House, he was walking his horse down the Main Street of Jensen Flats. The town, though small, was important in that part of Wyoming as the trading centre of several hundred miles of territory. On the main street, there were perhaps fifty buildings, some brick, some frame, and by far the most prosperous was the saloon.

The town was busy in the late afternoon. Drummers fresh from the Cheyenne stage which still ran despite people beginning to prefer the railroad, carried around their bags of samples. Men in bib overalls thronged the boardwalks. There were women of all ages, some in working dresses covered with canvas aprons, others sporting fine dresses from Cheyenne. Carlsen reached the sheriff's office, swung down from his saddle, and hitched his horse to the rail.

Sheriff Frank Fenner looked up from his desk as Carlsen pushed open the door from the street. 'Howdy, Jack. Coffee's good an' hot.'

'I'll take that, thanks.' Carlsen crossed the office and filled a mug from the metal pot that stood on the pot-bellied stove.

'So what brings you to town?'

Carlsen sat in the chair opposite the desk. 'We got

26

rustlers runnin' off our beef.'

'So catch 'em an' hang 'em,' he said.

'That's what I tol' the new owner.'

'I heard she's a real pretty lady from back east. I guess she's a mite on the gentle side an' that's why you're here.'

For a moment Carlsen was tempted to tell Fenner she wasn't on the gentle side at all, but that would give the wrong impression to someone who was yet to meet her.

'I reckon so,' he said.

'Jack, you look out on Main Street an' you'll see it's quiet. Folks go about their business, the homesteaders bring in their wagons every coupla weeks, the loggers come in from the forest on a Saturday night an' spend their money in the saloon. I throw a couple of 'em in the jail when they get to fightin' and kick 'em out on Sunday morning. An' that's it. If I want a real challenge I chase a few brats into the school-room. I'm gonna call it a day come the end o' summer an' that's the way I like it.' Fenner leaned back in his chair. 'You unn'erstand what I'm sayin'? Jensen Flats is quiet an' I aim to keep it thataways. The Bar Circle ain't no concern o' mine, an' that's the truth.'

'S'posin' those no-goods around the saloon have a hand in the rustlin'?'

Fenner put down his mug. 'Jack, I'll tell you somethin' about that passel of owl hoots. A coupla weeks after Bart Mason came to town and bought the Dollar, two of his no-goods drew on each other right in the damned middle of Main Street. Noon on Sunday, folks due to come outta church an' I had a body in the street.'

'So what did you do?'

'I went out to throw the shootist into jail. He draws on me, the damn fool, and now I got two bodies in the street. Took a hell of a clean-up afore the reverend finished his sermon.'

27

'How did Mason handle it?'

'I went to see him an' tol' him that I got thirty-two square miles to take care of, an' anythin' like that happened agin, I'd close down the Dollar an' chase all the men on his payroll outta town. An' it worked. I got the quietest town in the county.' Fenner hesitated. 'I'd like to help but I got one deputy who's gonna quit anytime now an' a tradin' town to look after. Anyways, you know the judge. He'd never convict a rustler, too damned difficult.'

Carlsen nodded. 'I was told to ask, that's all. Somethin' else. You heard Hendrix ran off the nester, name o' Ford?'

'I heard that.' Fenner looked across the desk with intelligent eyes. 'You connectin' Hendrix with losin' your beef?'

'He's land-hungry an' he's got the Bar Circle in his sights.'

'What's your reckonin'? Hendrix tryin' to gain from a gentlewoman comin' in as the new owner?'

'That's been on my mind. I ain't gonna let it happen.'

Fenner breathed in deeply. 'You start a range war an' it's gonna spill over on to the town. I ain't plannin' on cowboys shootin' up Main Street. Anyways, I thought you were done with gunfightin' years back.'

Carlsen nodded. 'So did I,' he said softly.

CHAPTER THREE

Carlsen took his breakfast at the Chinaman's place four buildings along from the billiards parlour in Main Street. After seeing Fenner the previous evening, it had been too late to carry on any business. He ate supper at the German's chophouse and then spent a couple of hours playing poker with the three ex-cavalrymen who ran the livery. When the four men had played their last hands, the ex-soldiers had found him a bunk for the night.

Now, walking along the boardwalk, he put a forefinger to the brim of his hat.

'Good morning, Eliza.'

Eliza Parsons, who had confounded the whole town by not remarrying after her husband had been killed at Gettysburg, returned his smile. 'Good morning, Jack. I hear we have a famous lady at the Bar Circle.'

'I guess you heard wrong, Eliza. What we have is a new lady owner.'

'Yes, Miss Jane Nicholls. She's a famous author back east.'

'She writes books?'

'Yes, indeed. Mr Kurtz has been telling me she's very successful.' Carlsen pursed his lips in a silent whistle, and Eliza showed a broad smile, obviously delighted at bringing news to her friend. 'Shall we be seeing her in town? Lots of folk

29

are keen to meet her. You must tell her about the town's dance.'

'I'll tell her but I ain't sure she'll make the time.' His mouth twitched. 'I guess there's somethin' surprisin' every day, Eliza.'

'Mrs Kurtz is hoping Miss Nicholls will give a talk to our Ladies Society.'

'I reckon she'll do that.' He touched the brim of his hat. 'Good day, Eliza, I must be about my business.'

He couldn't resist a backward glance at the attractive widow. Older than his new owner, of course, but Eliza still boasted a trim figure and a clear complexion. Maybe if he hadn't. . . . He mentally shook himself. A cold beer would chase away crazy thoughts.

He walked across Main Street to the saloon. Right now, after all the whiskey he'd drunk the previous evening, a glass of cold beer would taste just fine. No-good or not, Mason ran a fine saloon, and at this time of the day it should be quiet as the gamblers and the calico queens didn't show until nightfall. He stepped up to the boardwalk and pushed through the batwing doors. Half a dozen men sat at a table over to his right. Behind the bar, the barkeep was polishing a glass on a blue cloth. Otherwise the place was empty. The barkeep looked up as Carlsen reached the bar.

'Howdy, Mr Carlsen, it's been a while.'

'Howdy, Josh. I've been busy. New owner of the Bar Circle an' all. I'll take a beer.'

'Word has it she's a real pretty lady,' the barkeep said, drawing the beer. He pushed across the brimming glass to Carlsen.

'Word soon gets around,' Carlsen said. He put a coin on the bar and raised his glass in the direction of a table. 'I'm gonna take the weight off my feet.'

He'd been sitting at the table, turning over in his mind the problem of how to tackle the rustlers when the doors were pushed open and the morning sunlight was thrown on to the sawdust-covered floor. Carlsen looked across to see Hector Davis standing a few feet inside the saloon, looking around. His expression appeared to show Davis was satisfied with what he saw and he walked across to the bar, seemingly oblivious of the guffaws from the group of men over to the right of Carlsen.

'A whiskey, please,' Carlsen heard him say, aware that Davis hadn't noticed him sitting close to the wall.

He looked across to the group of men who were bent forward across their table, speaking in low tones to each other. They leaned back suddenly, sniggering over something that had just been said. One of the men, a Colt on his hip, and fancy stitching on his vest, stood up.

'See what happens, Will,' urged one.

Will walked across to the bar. 'Howdy, stranger,' he greeted Davis.

'Er, howdy.'

'Stranger comes into the Silver Dollar an' it's the custom to buy a man a whiskey.'

'Oh, OK.' Davis put his hand in his vest pocket and put a coin on the bar.

'Barman, give this gentleman a whiskey.'

Expressionless, the barkeep poured a whiskey and pushed it across. Will raised the glass and downed the whiskey. He looked across to the table where the men were watching, big grins on their faces. He turned back to Davis.

'That's a mighty fine hat you're wearin', stranger. I reckon you should give me that hat, sorta gift from a stranger to a man o' this town.'

Davis frowned. 'I can't see to do that.'

Will's hand shot out, pulling down the broad-brimmed

31

Stetson over Davis's eyes. 'Reckon you can't see anythin' now, stranger.'

A howl of laughter came from the men at the table, by which time Carlsen was halfway to the bar. 'OK, you've had your whiskey an' your fun, time you went back to your table.'

As Davis pushed up his hat, Will turned to face Carlsen. 'This is none o' your business, cowboy. You wanna watch your mouth or I'll shut it for you.'

Carlsen took two more strides and the sharp toe of his boot smashed into Will's kneecap. There was a crack of bone and an agonized cry as Will attempted to reach for his side-arm as he fell to the sawdust. Carlsen slammed down his boot on the man's wrist. He froze as he heard the metal-lic clicks of side-arms being cocked from behind him.

'Mr Carlsen ain't carryin'!'

Josh held a scatter-gun, aiming at the group of men around the table. 'I swear I'll blast all of you. Now sit down, an' let Mr Carlsen an' his friend just walk outta here.'

Carlsen felt his muscles relax. He bent down, pulled out Will's side-arm and stood up to slide the weapon along the bar. He looked down at Will, who glared up at him, his face red with fury.

'You try an' pull a gun on me again, an' I'm carryin', you're gonna end up dead,' Carlsen said evenly. He turned around to Davis. 'Reckon we ain't too welcome here.' He turned on his heel and with Davis alongside him, walked across the saloon and pushed through the doors. Behind them nobody moved.

'I'll do my drinking at the ranch,' Davis said. 'My buggy is along the street.'

'First, you're comin' with me.'

'Where are we going?' Davis asked, puzzled.

Instead of replying, Carlsen crossed the street, steering

Davis along the boardwalk to enter the General Store. In the shadowy interior, a young boy was polishing a brass lamp alongside a plump, red-faced man, with mutton-chop whiskers.

'Howdy, Mr Carlsen,' the red-faced man greeted him. 'You here to settle the account?'

'This gentleman, Mr Davis, takes care of the bills from now on,' Carlsen said. 'But first he needs some stuff.'

'I do?' Davis asked.

'Mr Rudman here is gonna find you two pairs of good pants, two good shirts, a leather vest, an' a hat. Your boots are fine, but he'll give you a pair o' Prairies for those fine Californian spurs you're wearin'.'

'Now look here, Carlsen?'

'An' while we're about it, Tom, get Mr Davis a pair o' workin' pants an' a workin' shirt.'

'That's enough, Carlsen! Even if I took the other stuff, what would I do with working clothes?'

'Cos from tomorrow you're gonna be movin' hay for a coupla hours every day.'

Davis exploded. 'Nonsense! You're a hired hand. You can't give me orders. My work is in the house with my books.'

'You'll have time for that. But you move hay until the fall an' we'll put some muscle on you. Afore you go east, you'll walk back into the Dollar an' kick that no-good's butt over the bar.'

Davis's mouth opened, the lawyer ready to bark out an objection. Then the frown of irritation on his face faded to be replaced by a hesitant smile. 'You think I could do that?'

'Sure, you could.'

'Then, heck, why not?' Davis turned to the store-keeper. 'I'll take the lot,' he said. He bent and unstrapped his Californian spurs, placing them on the counter. 'Put it all on the ranch account.'

The store-keeper looked uncomfortable. 'I'm sure the ranch is OK but. . . .' His voice trailed away.

Davis reached into his pocket and took out a thick wad of bills. 'I'll settle the account now in full. Just show me your book, and I'll need a copy the next time I'm in town.'

Carlsen was looking at the wad of notes. 'You always carry that around?'

'Why not?'

The store-keeper cleared his throat. 'Folks here are honest, Mr Davis, but we still got our passel o' wrong'uns. They take a look at that money you're carryin' an' they'll be after it.'

Davis hesitated, and then nodded. 'I guess you're right.' He handed over the whole stack of notes. 'Put that against the ranch account. Anything else you provide the ranch has to be signed for by me this summer. After we go back east, Mr Carlsen will sign as before.' He turned to Carlsen. 'JB wants me to go through the books, see how we're doin'.'

Carlsen nodded. 'Good thinkin'. James Nicholls wasn't slow to spend his money.' He took out his timepiece. 'We need to be gettin' back. Go get your buggy, an' while I think about it, you'd be better off with a horse.'

Carlsen and Davis were back at the ranch in time to greet Jane and Ethan on their return from riding out. While Davis went into the house to get changed, Carlsen stood in the yard as Jane and Ethan walked their horses across the yard to the front of the ranch-house. He took the bridle of the Appaloosa as Jane reined in and stepped down to the ground.

'How did it go, ma'am? Ethan was OK, I trust.'

Jane exchanged glances with the boy. 'Ethan was very good. He did everything I asked.' She brushed dust from her skirt with a gloved hand. 'Did you see the sheriff?'

Instead of replying, Carlsen turned to Ethan. 'Get the horses cleaned down and fed, an' then you an' Sean get somethin' to eat.'

He waited until Ethan had moved away before turning back to Jane.

'Yeah, I saw the sheriff. He said what I tol' you. The ranch takes care o' rustlers, he's too busy, an' even if he got 'em in front of a judge he'd never get a conviction.'

Her mouth set in a manner Carlsen was beginning to recognize. 'Then I shall—' She broke off, looking over Carlsen's shoulder. 'Who's this riding in?'

Carlsen turned. 'One of the Lazy Y boys, I reckon. Now what does he want?'

The rider reined his mount into a walk as he approached the ranch-house and halted as he drew alongside Carlsen and Jane. He stepped down from the saddle, tugging at the brim of his hat.

'Howdy, Miss Nicholls, Mr Carlsen. I've a message from Mr Hendrix. He asks if he and Mr Grant can pay a call early tomorrow afore they ride into town.'

'Thank you,' Jane said. 'We shall be pleased to see them. There's coffee if you have the time.'

'Thanks for the offer, ma'am, but I haveta get back.'

He tugged at his hat again, and stepped up to the saddle. Turning his mount's head, he trotted away from the ranch-house.

'I shall want you there when they call,' Jane said.

'I reckon you might find it useful if I tol' you about the Lazy Y and Walter Hendrix.'

Jane nodded. 'Come into the house in half an hour. We can talk in the small parlour.'

Carlsen stood up when Jane entered the small parlour. She might irritate the hell out of him but he still reckoned she

35

was the prettiest woman he'd seen in Wyoming. He paused until she had settled her skirts before taking his seat again.

'Walter Hendrix, I understand, owns the Lazy Y,' she said.

Carlsen used his thumb to scratch his cheek while marshalling his thoughts. He wasn't sure how to explain how her uncle had spent his time. He certainly didn't wish to explain how James Nicholls had died in a whore's bed in the Silver Dollar. Now it was more important to convince her of Hendrix's determination to get his hands on the Bar Circle. And although it stuck in his craw, he had to give her the best advice possible.

'You could sell the Bar Circle to Walter Hendrix tomorrow. He would try to beat down your price but if you stood firm he'd probably give you what you were asking for.'

'Did he make an offer to my uncle?'

'He did when your uncle first arrived here. Your uncle had notions about bein' a rancher but he found it hard goin'. When Hendrix saw how your uncle carried on, he reckoned he could sit back an' wait for the Bar Circle to fall into his hands.'

'I gather you had a poor opinion of my uncle.'

'He wasn't cut out for ranchin', ma'am.'

Her mouth twitched. 'We shall say no more about my late uncle. What is your own opinion of Hendrix?'

He's a land-hungry son of a bitch, Carlsen wanted to say, but he couldn't say that to a lady. 'The land of the Lazy Y was two ranches when your grandfather was alive. There was a ranch – the Double B – Hendrix got his hands on. Hired some no-goods to get what he wanted. He wants as much land as he can grab. If people get hurt it's not gonna worry him.'

'People like Ethan's family, you mean?'

'I reckon so, ma'am.'

36

Jane stood up, a determined expression on her face. 'I'll speak with Mr Davis about money. He handles all that for me. If Hendrix thinks he can run me off this ranch, owned by my family for three generations, he's badly mistaken.'

CHAPTER FOUR

Sean opened the door to Carlsen's cabin. 'Mr Hendrix's buggy an' a rider headin' our way, Mr Carlsen.'

'OK, Sean. I'll be along.'

He looked down again at the papers in front of him. The money he'd made before he gained peaceful work at the Bar Circle was sitting safe in a bank in Cheyenne, steadily gaining from interest the bank was paying. The money he earned from the Bar Circle was with the bank in Jensen. If Jane Nicholls did sell the ranch he'd have enough money to last him a while. He was healthy and vigorous. He'd changed his life once, he could do it again. He got up from his chair, stuffed the papers into a leather bag he kept for the purpose, and went out to meet the Hendrix father and son.

Walter Hendrix stepped from his buggy. Close up he was a mountain of a man. Years earlier, he would have out-muscled most men in the county but since his wife's death several years before, he'd got fat, having gained a reputation for eating huge steaks washed down with beer chased with expensive whiskey. He wore a grey Stetson matched with a broadcloth grey suit, and highly polished brown boots. Hendrix gestured to his son, who was swinging down from his saddle, easing the unusual red-coloured reins he favoured.

'Howdy, Carlsen. You know Grant.'

'Howdy, Mr Hendrix.'

Carlsen exchanged nods with the younger Hendrix. Their rivalry at the annual shooting contest had once tipped over into a barroom brawl, and only the town mayor stepping in had saved one or the other from a serious beating. They met on occasion to discuss cattle business and while both appeared to have put their brawling behind them, Carlsen was aware of the threat to the Bar Circle provided by Grant Hendrix.

'You wanna come this way, Mr Hendrix. Soon as we're settled, Mrs Gittins will have coffee for us.'

Hendrix frowned. 'You're sitting in with us?'

'Sure am, Mr Hendrix. So's Mr Davis, Miss Jane's business manager.'

'Business manager? What the heck's that? All this for a courtesy call?'

Carlsen didn't reply directly. 'Follow me, an' I'll take you through.'

Inside the house, Jane was seated in the big parlour, accompanied by Hector Davis who stood up as the men entered and exchanged greetings.

'We reckoned we'd drop by and welcome you to Jensen Flats, Miss Nicholls,' Hendrix said when everyone was seated. 'I hope you'll be attending the dance in town next month.'

'An' that you'll save me a dance,' Grant added.

Jane smiled in his direction. 'How delightful. I do like to dance with someone who knows how to waltz and two-step.'

Grant hesitated. 'I don't lay claim to them dances, ma'am, but I do enjoy a quadrille.'

'Oh yes, I recall that boisterous dance. So tiring.' Jane picked up a small bell and rang it a couple of times. A few moments later, the housekeeper and Lucy entered the room. Each carried a tray bearing fine china cups and saucers, and a pot of coffee.

'Thank you, Mrs Gittins.' Jane looked across at Walter Hendrix. 'Would you care for some coffee, Mr Hendrix?'

'Thank you.' He held out his left hand and took the coffee from Lucy.

'I'll take coffee,' said Grant.

Carlsen refused the offer. He was more interested in how Grant Hendrix was going to handle the small cup. Lucy brought across coffee and placed the cup and saucer in front of Jane. Davis took his cup from Mrs Gittins.

'Mr Carlsen tells me you made an offer to my uncle for this ranch, Mr Hendrix.'

'That's correct, ma'am, but I'm no longer interested.'

'Yes, I suppose you have enough range now that the nesters have left.'

'A good rancher can always use more land.'

'I'm told that Mr Ford and his family have joined a wagon train. Is that why he sold you the cattle so cheaply?'

'I gave the nester a fair price.'

Jane sipped her coffee. 'Maybe I've misunderstood.' She looked across at Carlsen. 'Didn't Ethan say he'd seen the bill of sale?'

Carlsen had no idea if Ethan had seen a bill of sale, but he was inwardly chuckling at Hendrix growing redder in the face by the second.

'Sure did, ma'am,' he said, poker-faced. 'He was surprised his pa sold his stock for so little money.'

Jane nodded thoughtfully. 'Yes, I imagine Mr Ford was under considerable pressure.' She paused. 'Being so keen to join the wagon-train, I mean.'

'Who's this Ethan you're talkin' about?' Grant Hendrix asked.

'Ford's eldest son,' Carlsen said. 'He stayed behind an' I've taken him on. He'll be useful when we put some of our stock on land he knows.'

'Hold it there, Carlsen,' Walter Hendrix barked. 'I've put the stock I bought on that land.'

'But that's open range, Mr Hendrix,' Jane said. 'Anyone can put stock on that grass.'

'You put your beef with ours,' Grant snapped, 'an' that could start trouble between the men.'

Jane looked around the room, wide-eyed with apparent surprise. 'But I thought that was why we branded the cattle. So there'd be no disputes.'

Walter Hendrix looked at his son. Carlsen could see that Walter Hendrix knew he wasn't going to get very far with Jane Nicholls. Would he come right out in the open and make an offer for the Bar Circle? If he thought the ranch was heading for financial ruin, he might choose to stay his hand and be content to ride in and pick up the pieces. But maybe Jane Nicholls had upset his plans. Anyone listening to her, with her convincing display of an owner confident in the future of her ranch, would not suspect that the Bar Circle was in need of investment.

'But, Mr Hendrix, I do understand that more cattle means a need for more grass,' Jane said. 'I'm only sorry that Mr Ford didn't give me the chance to buy his stock as I intend to invest more in the Bar Circle. There are people in England who are keen to follow Lord Frewen's example.' She looked directly at Walter Hendrix. 'Had you ever considered selling the Lazy Y? I'd be willing to make an offer.'

The atmosphere in the parlour suddenly chilled. A blue vein bulged at the side of Hendrix's head and his mouth opened as he struggled for words. The total silence was only broken by the coughing and spluttering of Davis, who pulled a silk handkerchief from his pocket and held it to his mouth.

'Do forgive me,' he said when he managed to speak. 'The coffee was hotter than I expected.'

'Two generations of the Hendrix family have owned the Lazy Y,' Hendrix said curtly, finding his voice. 'My son here will be the third in the years to come.'

'Then we shall have something in common,' Jane said, turning to Grant Hendrix with a smile. 'Well, almost,' she added, 'as I'm the fourth generation of Nicholls to own the Bar Circle.' She looked at Walter Hendrix. 'We must meet again soon and discuss any problems. Mr Carlsen tells me that some of our cattle have been driven away. I hate the thought of hanging men, but after all, rustlers are nothing more than common thieves.' She smiled sweetly. 'Now do forgive me, gentlemen, Mrs Gittins will be serving lunch. And I do look forward to that dance, if we can find the time to attend,' she said to Grant Hendrix. 'Oh, but I remember, you don't waltz or two-step. Such a pity.'

She swept from the room, as the men struggled to their feet. Carlsen stood there poker-faced, not looking at Davis. Had he done so, he would have burst out laughing.

Carlsen finished his midday meal, his recollections of the Hendrix visit still prompting smiles. Jane Nicholls was turning out to be a woman, the like of whom hadn't been seen before in Jensen Flats. Were all the young women like this back east? Sassy and quick-thinking? Maybe he'd be on safer ground if he abandoned notions of taking the UP.

He sure wasn't intent on marrying any of the calico queens down at the Dollar but at least they didn't get sassy with him. The feisty manner in which his new boss had dealt with the Hendrix father and son without ever being other

42

than a fine lady had been something to see.

The grin was still on his face as he walked across to the horse-barn. Sean was busy pumping water while Ethan was brushing the coat of a chestnut, already saddled. The leathers gleamed and the afternoon sun throwing its rays through the barn door sparkled on the metal bars of the stirrups.

'Who's ridin' the chestnut?' Carlsen asked. 'I reckon that's a mite too much horseflesh for Mr Davis.'

Sean and Ethan exchanged glances and both laughed aloud. Carlsen frowned. 'You two ain't setting him up, I hope. Mr Davis is OK.'

Sean shook his head. 'I've got the little mare for Mr Davis. Sweet as candy.' He patted the neck of the chestnut. 'This beauty is for Miss Jane. She came over from the house an' rode him around the yard. Said he suited her, an' I was to have him ready so she an' Ethan can ride an' see some more of the ranch.'

'So where's her side-saddle?'

'She tol' me she didn't need it,' Ethan said.

'You two wait here. I'll tell you when to bring Miss Jane's horse,' Carlsen said sharply. He swung on his heel and went striding across to the house. He was five yards from the steps leading to the door when the door opened and Jane Nicholls appeared.

Carlsen stopped in his tracks. She wore corduroy riding pants tucked into high leather boots. Silver spurs, Plains-style, gleamed in the sun. Above the corduroy pants ,she wore a dark brown, leather trail jacket over a cotton shirt and around her fair hair was folded a silk square.

'Is anything wrong, Mr Carlsen? And where is my horse?'

Carlsen mentally shook himself. Another side of Jane Nicholl's character had surprised him. Was this the way young ladies back east were conducting themselves? If the ladies of the town saw her dressed in this manner, wealthy or not, they'd mark her down as a hussy. Should he say anything? Then he immediately kicked that notion over a five-bar gate. She'd most likely chew his head off.

'I was checkin' with Sean that you'd given up on the side-saddle,' he said, as evenly as he could. 'You could find the change a mite tricky.'

Jane Nicholls sighed loudly. 'Mr Carlsen, there are schools in Boston that have been teaching your style of riding for over twenty years. I've been attending one such school for over six months.'

Then your demand for a side-saddle, Miss Jane Nicholls, was just to show us who is boss, Carlsen thought. But he didn't say it. He reminded himself he needed to get along with this feisty young woman.

'I'd like Sean to ride with you today, if you're OK with that.'

'Yes, that would be fine.'

'He'll have the chestnut here pronto,' he said. He turned on his heel and retraced to the barn where Sean and Ethan were waiting for their orders.

'You'll ride with Miss Jane, today, Sean. You act proper when you're with her and don't keep looking at her legs.'

Carlsen grinned at Sean's puzzled frown.

'Miss Jane's in smart ridin' pants.'

'Jumpin' rattlesnakes! Makes sense, though, she gonna ride 'cross the horse.'

Ten minutes later, Jane Nicholls and Sean, who had hastily donned fresh pants and a shirt, rode away from the house. Carlsen watched them go, seeing that his new boss sat across the chestnut as if she'd never ridden in a different style. When the hands up with the beef saw her, they'd reckon that the Fourth of July had come a month earlier.

He turned to Ethan. 'OK, back to the barn. I got questions

44

fer you.' He followed the boy, who faced him in the barn with a look of apprehension.

'You wanna keep workin' here?' Carlsen asked sharply.

'Sure I do, Mr Carlsen.' Ethan's smile faded. 'Have I done somethin' wrong?'

'Somethin' happened yesterday. You been soundin' off to Miss Jane about your kinfolk bein' chased off their land?'

'I never said a word.' He hesitated. 'That is until . . .' Ethan's voice trailed away.

'Until what?'

'Miss Jane had already heard about Pa quittin' an' asked me to show her where we'd had our shanty.'

'An' what did you say?'

'I tol' Miss Jane I couldn't do that cos you'd tol' me I wasn't to go there.'

'OK, you did right.'

Ethan looked away from Carlsen. 'But that ain't the end of it. Miss Jane said she's the owner of the ranch an' I had to do what she tol' me. An' I was to take her there.'

'An' you did, I s'pose.'

Ethan bit his lip. 'Yes, boss.'

Carlsen nodded. 'OK, Ethan, keep workin' on that saddle.'

He turned on his heel and strode across to the ranch-house. He flung open the door, his hat remaining on his head, surprising Mrs Gittins who was crossing the hall from one of the parlours.

'My, my, Jack. You look flustered,' she said.

'As soon as Miss Jane returns, I wanna have a word with her.'

The house-keeper nodded, seemingly reluctant to ask questions. 'I'll tell her if you're not around.'

Carlsen spent two or three hours studying more papers in his cabin. If the ranch was to survive he knew they had to spend money. Repairs were needed for the Big House, new timber for the corrals, and they'd be wise to hire hands to dig another well. He'd just decided that he had to join forces with Hector Davis when the door to his cabin burst open. Ethan stood in the doorway, his face pale.

'Mr Carlsen, you gotta come quick.'

Carlsen looked up. 'You got trouble with the horses, Ethan? Sean will be back soon. He'll handle it.'

'No, no, boss! It's Miss Jane?'

Carlsen was on his feet in an instant. 'OK, I'm on my way.'

With four long strides he was out of the cabin and on to the hardpack surrounding the house.

'What the hell?'

Approaching the house at a slow walk was Jane's chestnut carrying both Jane and Sean. On a loose rein, Sean's horse followed behind. Sean's arms were around Jane's waist and his wrists were loosely tied to prevent him from falling from the horse. As the horse drew closer, both Carlsen and Ethan broke into a run towards them. Carlsen could see the blood staining the shoulder of Jane's jacket.

Carlsen pointed towards the blacksmith's lean-to. 'Bring that handcart over, an' make it quick,' he ordered Ethan. Ten more yards and he was alongside the chestnut, Jane staring down at him white-faced. 'Somebody shot Sean. We were by the river and. . . .' Her voice broke, and she swallowed furiously.

'OK, ma'am. I'll handle it.'

He leaned over and loosened the silk scarf from around Sean's wrists that he'd last seen covering Jane's hair. As he did so, Ethan arrived with the handcart.

'OK, we're gonna get Sean on to the cart, and take him to my cabin. There's a spare bunk there.'

Taking care not to brush against Sean, Jane dismounted.

'Take him to the house, Mr Carlsen,' she said. 'He'll be more comfortable there.'

Carlsen nodded. 'OK. We'll walk the chestnut to the house. Ethan, take charge of Sean's horse.' He took hold of Sean's arm. 'Sean, you hear me?'

A slurred voice muttered, 'Yes, boss.'

'We're gonna get you off this horse when we get to the house. It's gonna hurt but we gotta do it sometime.'

There was a noise from Sean which Carlsen took to mean Sean knew what was going on. Slowly, they walked the chestnut across the hardpack until they'd reached the house. Carlsen pushed hard against the horse's side to put his arm around Sean's waist.

'OK, Sean, here we go.'

Bunching the muscles in his legs, Carlsen allowed Sean to slide off the horse and against him, before turning to cradle him in his arms like a child. Save for a muffled groan, Sean remained silent until Carlsen had carried him up the wide stairs.

'He was in the cottonwoods, boss,' Sean said in a weak voice.

'Take it easy, Sean. I'll handle that,' Carlsen said, his breathing heavy.

'Put him in your old room, Mr Carlsen.'

Twenty minutes later, with the help of Hector Davis, the wounded man had been put in Carlsen's old bed, his clothes stripped, and Mrs Gittins, after telling Carlsen that Sean wouldn't be the first young man she'd seen without his pants, had cleaned the wound with warm water and bound his chest with cloth torn from an old paillasse. Meanwhile, Jane had changed her clothes and she, Hector Davis and Carlsen were now seated in the small parlour.

'Shouldn't we have driven Sean into town?' Jane asked.

Carlsen shook his head. 'He'd never make it. Ethan's

47

taken the buggy an' will bring Doc Wilson.'

'If you'll excuse us, Jane,' Davis said in a tone that brooked no argument, 'Carlsen and I are going to have a whiskey.' Carlsen shook his head, but Davis went over to a table and poured himself a generous drink before he turned to Jane.

'I warned you before we came here that taking over a ranch would not be easy.'

'Nonsense, Hector. A hunter fires a stray shot, a man gets injured, and you think it's the end of the world.'

'No, ma'am. Mr Davis has it right. Yesterday, you made Ethan go back to where he'd been livin',' Carlsen said brusquely. 'I'd told Ethan he was not to do that.'

'But I told him he could, Mr Carlsen.' Her eyes sparkled. 'I own this ranch and pay Ethan his wages. If I give him an order, he will obey it. What happened yesterday has nothing to do with the shooting today.'

'We don't know that for sure, Miss Jane. Maybe Hendrix was sending a warning that you'd be better off selling the Bar Circle to him.'

Jane looked at Hector Davis. 'Do you think that's possible?'

Davis looked thoughtful. 'Hendrix wants this ranch, whatever he's said. He may see you as a threat to his plans.'

Jane's eyes widened. 'Do you mean. . . ?'

'This shooting business could mean just that,' Carlsen cut in. 'The shootist wasn't aimin' to kill Sean. He was trying to kill you.'

CHAPTER FIVE

'That buggy driver of yours sure knows how to make a fast journey,' said Dr Wilson wryly, as he stepped into the Big House. He wore a battered grey city suit and carried a new Stetson in his hand. 'Scared the pants off me.' His smile faded and was replaced with a look of determination. 'Where's this feller Sean?'

'Upstairs, Doctor,' Jane said. 'Mr Carlsen will show you the way.'

'This way, Doc,' Carlsen said, leading Wilson up the stairs and along the short corridor to his old room. Sean lay on his back, his eyes closed, on the narrow bed in the corner of the room. Beside him, Mrs Gittins stood up from her chair as the two men entered. Over her normal working dress she wore a canvas apron.

Wilson opened the black bag he was carrying and placed it on a nearby table. He took a long look at Sean, as if judging the situation.

'OK, let's see what we got. Help me turn him over, Jack.'

As gently as he was able, aware of Sean's groan of pain, Carlsen lifted Sean's shoulder, and together the two men turned Sean over on to his stomach.

'Am I gonna die, Mr Carlsen?' Sean's weak voice was muffled against the coarse material of the pillow.

'No, you ain't gonna die, Sean,' Carlsen said urgently. 'You listen to me! Miss Jane's got you back here, an' you ain't gonna let her down by dyin'. One day I reckon you're gonna be runnin' the beef for the Bar Circle. You unn'er-stand?'

Sean gave a brief nod and then closed his eyes. His head became heavier on the pillow. Mrs Gittins's hand went to her mouth.

'Oh, my god,' she whispered. 'Have we lost him?'

Wilson shook his head. 'Miss Jane got him back in time. The bullet's almost gone through him but I'll get that out and keep the wound clean, an' he'll be fine. But it'll take time. I'm gonna have to check if there's bone damage in there.' He looked at Carlsen. 'I'll need Mrs Gittins to stay and give me a hand, and I'll want you later when we move him. After I'm done here we'll take him back to town.'

'I reckon Miss Jane will be fine if you want to keep him here.'

'No, it's better if I can keep a close watch on him.'

'OK, I'll let Miss Jane know what's goin' on.'

As Carlsen reached the bottom of the stairs, he saw Jane standing in the open doorway of the small parlour. He fol-lowed her into the room but was then taken aback when she swung around to face him.

'My God! You're all animals!' Twin patches of red showed on her cheekbones and her mouth was set in a hard line. 'Sean could die before his life has even begun.'

'Listen, Miss Jane! Sean's not gonna die. That was smart thinkin' to put a wad o' cloth over the wound. Now let's just sit down an' you can tell me what happened.'

For a few moments she glared at him, at one point opening her mouth to say more. Then Carlsen saw her relax and she sat down in the soft chair by the open fire-place.

'Yes, you're right,' she said, her voice almost under control. 'I'm being foolish. This isn't New York. Grandpa Jackson would be ashamed of me.'

Carlsen took the chair opposite and asked the question that had been burning in his gullet ever since he'd first seen Sean and Jane riding towards the ranch-house.

'Did you go near the nester's old place?'

'No, we were miles from there. Maybe only half a mile from the river. We thought about riding up to see Blackie and the men but by then, time was getting on and I had work to do.'

'So where were you when Sean was shot?'

'Somewhere close to the stand of cottonwoods where the river bends. Sean was talking about reporting to you on the state of the river banks. At first I couldn't understand what had happened. I heard a sound which I realize now must have been a gun being fired and then Sean just fell from his horse with blood oozing from his shoulder.' She shuddered at the memory. 'I thought it was rustlers at first.'

'Did you see anyone?'

'Nobody. I was so frightened I grabbed Sean's Winchester and fired at the cottonwoods. I knew I was unlikely to hit anyone but I thought a shot might show I was ready to fight.'

Carlsen sat up straight in his chair with surprise. 'How in tarnation did you know how to do that?'

'Ethan showed me yesterday when we rode up to see Blackie. He said I was a fine shot – a good eye or something.' She looked thoughtful. 'I realize Hendrix is ruthless about gaining more land but would he really hire an assassin?'

'I don't know,' Carlsen said grimly. 'But I aim to find out.'

*

Carlsen left the house and walked back to his cabin. He knelt beside his bunk and pulled out a large wooden box. He put aside a couple of books and the spare pants and shirts he kept packed, before pulling out a battered tin box containing all sorts of junk he'd thought worth keeping over the years and would probably throw away one day when he was feeling in the mood. His hands finally brushed the smooth leather of his gun belt and he pulled it free from the rest of his bits and pieces. Then he took out a large mahogany box and placed it on the bunk alongside the gun belt.

For a moment, he considered putting the box and the belt back below his spare clothes again and riding into Jensen to tell Fenner what had happened with Sean. But he guessed the sheriff would say he had a town to look after, and the shooting hadn't happened within the thirty-two square miles of his territory.

Carlsen opened the box and looked down on the Navy Colt, nestling in the green baize. Alongside the sidearm was space for a pocket pistol and Carlsen reminded himself that he needed to replace the one mislaid last year at the annual shooting contest.

The blue-black metal of the Colt's barrel gleamed in the sun, reaching into the cabin, and the ivory of the butt was as white as fresh milk. When he'd first come to the ranch, he'd cleaned the Colt carefully each week, telling himself for a while that he was only keeping the sidearm in perfect condition, should he ever wish to sell it.

That was before he'd decided to enter the annual shooting held in Jensen. Since then the competition had developed into a three-way contest between himself, William Kurtz, the town's lawyer, who'd been a major in the Union Army, and Grant Hendrix. Thoughts of shooting prompted him to think more about Hendrix. But if Grant

Hendrix had attempted to shoot either Jane or Sean, he wouldn't have made a mistake. He was as good with a long gun as he was with a sidearm.

Carlsen picked up the belt and buckled it around his waist. Then he slid the Colt into his holster. He didn't need the practice but he drew the weapon several times before he was satisfied. Fenner was right. Trouble on a ranch was best dealt with by the ranch. He needed to get a handle on exactly what was going on. When he discovered who was behind the attempt on Jane's life, even if he hadn't pulled the trigger himself, he'd kill the son of a bitch.

Three hours later, he hitched his palomino to the rail in front of Fenner's office and stepped up to the sheriff's door. If there was going to be shooting then he wanted to make sure Fenner knew what was going on. Folks in the town might pick up a gun to go hunting but aside from the no-goods in Mason's saloon, there wasn't a man who'd shoot at a fellow human being. The sheriff had made it clear that he wanted a quiet time and he'd get real ornery if there was trouble in the town.

'Howdy, Jack. There's coffee in the pot.' He glanced at the Colt on Carlsen's hip. 'You on the Meadow early this year?'

Carlsen ignored the offer of coffee. 'Some sonovabitch bushwhacked one o' my hands. Doc Wilson is out at the Bar Circle now. Sean Docherty ain't yet sixteen, an' he don't deserve to die.'

'Why would anyone bushwhack a young feller?'

Carlsen thought for a moment. Could he trust Fenner to keep his mouth shut? If he were to tell him that maybe Jane had been the target, how would Fenner react? If the word got around that some no-good had attempted to kill a ranch-owner it could gain the town a reputation for lawlessness, and that wouldn't sit easily with Fenner.

'Sean was ridin' with Miss Nicholls. I think she was the target.'

Fenner put down his coffee and kicked forward his chair. 'Fer chris'sakes! Don't you talk about that in town.'

'I'm not gonna say a word. We told Doc Wilson to say Sean was out ridin' on his own, an' he's given me his word he'll say nothin'.'

Fenner blew air out of pursed lips. 'So why you tellin' me this if you wanna keep folks from knowin'?'

'You ain't gonna tell anyone, I guess. But I find the bush-whacker in town an' you're gonna have some shootin'.'

Fenner breathed in deeply. 'Hell! I shoulda known life was too quiet.'

Carlsen left his horse outside the sheriff's office and walked along the boardwalk to the General Store. The arrival of good weather meant that the town was at last waking up from the long winter. Main Street was drying out and townsfolk were leaving their slickers at home. Men bustled around, discussing business, carrying tools to the blacksmith, and driving wagons loaded with sacks of seeds. The many years the town had been established meant that there were plenty of women to be seen bustling in and out of stores, others deep in conversation with their neigh-bours. Carlsen turned into the store to see Rudman behind the counter, head down, scribbling on a sheet of paper.

'Tom, I need some slugs for my Colt.'

Rudman stood up, glancing at Carlsen's sidearm. 'You startin' in the Meadow early this year?'

'No, I ain't.' Carlsen walked over to a shelf at the side of the store and took down four boxes. 'These'll be fine. You got a throwin' knife?'

'Fer chris'sakes, Jack. I thought you were in the ranchin' business now. I hope you ain't aimin' to start a war in

Jensen.' Rudman sounded anxious. 'The town's been quiet for a long while.'

'Don't worry. The trouble's out at the ranch. I ain't aimin' to start anythin' in town.'

'What sorta trouble?'

'Some shootist bushwhacked one o' my hands.'

Rudman blew a silent whistle. He held up a slim seven-inch knife. 'This what you're lookin' for?'

'That'll do fine. Gotta sheath an' a saddle string? An' I'll take one o' your pocket pistols. That fancy one you sold me a coupla years back seems to have disappeared.'

'I'll get Mrs Rudman.'

It was something of a joke in the town that Rudman's second wife handled the gun business for the store. As a young woman before the War, she'd fought Apaches alongside her kinfolk. Her first appearance at the annual shooting contest had meant red faces among some of the men when she'd showed how she handled a Winchester.

While Carlsen was waiting for Mrs Rudman to appear, he walked over to where Rudman had an open case, showing half a dozen pocket pistols. He was examining them when a door opened behind the counter.

'Well, Jack Carlsen, ain't that happenstance!' Mrs Rudman stood in the doorway. 'I was checkin' stock only yesterday.'

She held up a pocket pistol. 'Musta been a matchin' pair I bought a while back. You bought one and this got shoved under some boxes.' She showed Carlsen the .22, turning the pistol over so the small circle of coloured glass set in the butt was exposed. 'Same as you bought for the shootin' contest.'

'I'll take it,' Carlsen said. 'Don't put my stuff on the books. I'll pay cash.'

'Sure thing, Jack. Good to do business.'

The Rudmans watched as Carlsen slid the knife into its sheath which settled with a silky whisper. He pushed back his vest and shirt at the nape of his neck and looped the string around his neck, allowing the sheath to fall beneath his shirt, covered underneath his leather vest.

'You gonna tell us what's going on at the Bar Circle?' Tom Rudman asked.

Carlsen looked at the couple for a second. 'Some no-good reckons he can bring trouble to us at the ranch. He's gonna learn that he shoulda found another line o' business.'

The saloon was deserted, save for Josh behind the bar and a couple of calico queens seated against the wall opposite the bar, playing cards. They looked up as Carlsen crossed the saloon.

'Hiya, Jack,' a fair-haired girl said. 'You don't come an' see us anymore.'

'Brandin' time,' he said. 'You know how it is.' He looked towards the stairs. 'Is Mason upstairs?'

'Yeah, but he don't like bein' hassled,' the young woman said.

'Who said anythin' about hasslin'?'

'I'm lookin' at you, Jack. You're gonna hassle him.'

Carlsen put out his hand and lightly held her chin. 'Guess you know me better than myself, Tex,' he said with a grin.

He dropped his hand and walked away from the two women, the grin disappearing from his face after a couple of paces. He climbed the stairs, and settled his gun belt as he reached the corridor. He'd been up here a few times and knew the saloon owner had his office at the end of the corridor. He reached Mason's door and pushed it open.

'Don't you ever knock?'

Mason sat behind a mahogany desk. He wore a dark blue Prince Albert jacket which was open to reveal a soft green vest over a silk shirt set off with a flowing yellow tie. He was clean-shaven, save for long sideburns which showed flecks of grey among the dark hair. Between his clenched teeth he held a thin cheroot.

Carlsen didn't reply. Instead he took the chair from beside the desk, and twirled it around. He then straddled the chair, staring at Mason. Still he said nothing.

Mason frowned. 'I got you now, Jack Carlsen, range boss out at the Bar Circle. What's the big idea, you stormin' in here?'

'I gotta make a decision,' Carlsen said.

'What the hell you talkin' about?'

'It's like this. The next coupla days, I'm gonna catch up with the no-good who bushwhacked one o' my hands. I gotta decide who I kill. Him or the sonovabitch who gave him his orders. But studying on it I reckon I'll kill the two of 'em.'

Mason tore at his cheroot, flinging it in the spittoon that sat beside his desk. His face was purple with anger. Spittle came from his mouth as he shouted.

'An' you're sayin' I got something to do with it? Are you goddamned crazy? Why should I wanna shoot some god-damned cowboy?'

'Try an' scare off the new owner, mebbe. Same as I heard your no-goods scared off the folks at the Double B.'

'For chris'sakes, Carlsen! That was a while back, and anyways, I had nothin' to do with that! An' I ain't been shootin' up your cowboys neither.' Mason sucked air into his lungs. 'Sure, I got some rough boys on my payroll. You come round on Saturday night when the men come in from the forest an' you'll see why. I got Josh at the bar an' the gals to look after. Make sure they don't get hurt. That's the way

57

I make my money.'

'So you reckon you ain't got a hand in the shootin'?'

Mason pulled his lips back from his teeth. 'If it was somebody on my payroll he's been hired without my knowin'. Fenner's told me more than once to stick to sellin' whiskey an' women or he'll close me down.'

Carlsen stared directly at him for several moments. Then he stood up.

'I haveta come back in here over this, you're gonna be in a passel of trouble.'

Carlsen crossed Main Street to walk to the livery. The big barn was set halfway down the street, along an alley which backed on to the Silver Dollar. The strains of a fiddle reached him as he turned into the alley. Some musician practising for the Saturday night crowd, he guessed. He entered the barn, the tang of horseflesh reaching his nostrils.

'Howdy, Jack,' Zeke Gale, the liveryman greeted him, ducking beneath the head of a roan. 'Good to see you in town again. What can I do for you?'

'I need a favour, Zeke. I need to hire your Shoshone for a coupla days. There's a trackin' job I gotta do.'

'You're lucky, Jack, we ain't too busy. I reckon we can make a deal. How's about a dollar a day for Charlie an' a dollar for me?'

'If he's as good a tracker as he is with horses it'll be a quick job. I'm obliged, Zeke.'

He pulled out coins from his vest pocket as Gale turned and called out.

'Charlie, down here!'

A big Shoshone, in bib overalls and moccasins, jumped down from the ledge on the barn where piles of straw were stacked. The sun threw light on to his mahogany coloured face and shoulders.

58

'I gotta trackin' job for you,' Gale said. 'You're gonna work for Mr Carlsen.'

The Shoshone nodded. 'OK, am I goin' far?'

'No more than a coupla days,' Carlsen said. 'You know the stand o' cottonwoods on the bend o' the river?'

The Shoshone nodded.

'Meet me near there after sun-up tomorrow. You got a coupla dollars comin' your way. But do a good job an' you'll be back by tomorrow nightfall.'

CHAPTER SIX

Charlie, the Shoshone, was leaning on the horn of his saddle when Carlsen arrived at the stand of cottonwoods a couple of hundred yards to the west of the river. He took care to approach the trees in a wide sweep so as not to spoil any tracks the Shoshone might find.

The Shoshone was wearing his old army jacket, the blue faded with the sun, the gold stripes worn as decoration rather than indicating rank. On his feet were leather moccasins, and above them he wore Plains spurs, an unusual habit for a Shoshone, which he must have acquired riding for several years with the army. His black hair which fell almost to his shoulders was topped with a wide-brimmed brown hat with a multi-colour band.

'G'mornin', Mr Carlsen. A fine day for trackin'.'

'Some bushwhacker shot one o' my hands yesterday,' Carlsen said. 'That don't set easy with me. I reckon he was in these cottonwoods. The ground's still hard but I'm hopin' you can find his tracks, an' tell me where he was headin' for.'

Charlie nodded. 'Best you leave it to me to take a look.'

'OK, I'm gonna check out the river banks.'

Carlsen turned the head of his palomino. There was no sense in getting under the Shoshone's feet while he was scouting around. There was always the chance he would find nothing. And although at this time of the year it wasn't usual for anyone from the ranch to ride up here, it was always possible that a stranger could have ridden across the spread, heading for Jensen Flats.

He reached the riverbank and saw that it remained firm despite the bad winter they'd been through. Memories of his first winter came back to him and caused him to smile. He thought he'd seen bad winters in Montana but he'd seen nothing until that first storm hit Wyoming. By the turn of that year when his whole life changed, he was ready to quit the cattle business. He figured that getting shot at was an easier ride than riding his horse through snow up to his spurs. Only Jackson Nicholls had persuaded him to stay, reminding him that all he had to go back to was a one way trip to Boot Hill. Full damned circle, he swore, as he swung down from his saddle, and lowered himself to the grass, hitching the palomino's reins to the ground root of a cottonwood.

He dropped to the grass, his thoughts turning over to what would happen if Jane had been killed. Would Hector Davis have been required to sell the Bar Circle? He hadn't asked himself that question before. Did Jane have a brother who would take over? It seemed unlikely or surely the ranch would have been handed down to him. Maybe there was no one else left in the close family, and if Jane didn't survive, then the ranch would be handed over to the lawyers to track down distant relatives. Carlsen's hand, held high to throw a pebble in the water, suddenly froze. Davis was a lawyer. Could he be behind all this trouble while playing at being the concerned friend? When a ranch was there for the taking lots of folks would be keen to make a quick dollar.

'Mr Carlsen! Hallooo!'

Carlsen scrambled to his feet, released the palomino's

reins, and stepped up to his saddle as heard the call from Charlie. Had he found something already? If so, he was worth another couple of dollars. He kicked on his mount, heading at a lope to where the Shoshone was sitting astride his pony close to the trees, a wide grin across his dark-skinned face.

'That was damned quick, Charlie.'

The Shoshone's teeth flashed. 'You got any more trackin' jobs? I'm hopin' they're as good.'

'You know where he was headin'?'

'Better than that. I can tell you who was shootin'.'

Carlsen grunted. 'You doin' Shoshone magic this mornin', Charlie?'

'Take a look at this, boss.'

Charlie turned his pony's head and walked his mount to the corner of the stand on the opposite side to the river, with Carlsen a few yards behind him.

The Shoshone slid from his saddle, and squatted on his heels. In his hand he held a stick which he pointed at the ground. Carlsen looked down. At first, all he could see was a tuft of bunch and buffalo grass. He stepped down from his saddle and, like the Shoshone, squatted on his heels.

'You see it now, boss?'

Was there a slight indentation on the grass? Carlsen wasn't sure. Charlie leaned forward and traced a shape with his finger. 'That's your bushwhacker's plate,' Charlie said.

'So where's he ridin' to?'

Charlie shrugged. 'It don't matter. There's a nick in the plate on the foreleg. Horse belongs to a feller named Mooney, works for Mr Mason at the saloon. He's been in the livery talkin' about getting it fixed. I guess you'll find him in town.' Charlie looked up as Carlsen stood. 'They say he's fast.'

'OK, I'll see you later.'

'I fancy havin' the money now, boss.' The Shoshone shrugged. 'Y'know, just in case he's faster than you.'

'Fer chris'sakes, Charlie!' Carlsen thrust his hand into his vest pocket. 'Two dollars, an' another two for doin' a good job.'

Carlsen walked his horse down Main Street. He reached Fenner's office and for a moment, considered calling on the sheriff and telling him what Charlie had found. If he found Mooney and got him to the sheriff, would Fenner take his word on what had happened to Miss Jane and Sean? Or would he just shrug and say it was nothing to do with him? But if there was shooting around the town, Fenner would get ornery. Carlsen turned over in his mind what he should do. To hell with it! He'd settle this business himself.

He reined in his mount as he reached the Silver Dollar and swung down from his saddle. The town was quiet, most folks having gone home for a meal. A brown dog, his tail held high, ran across the street and disappeared down an alleyway as if knowing that trouble was coming. Carlsen hitched up his gun belt and went up the steps to the saloon.

The place was empty, apart from Josh behind the bar and three men playing cards at a table in the centre of the room. Carlsen recognized one of the players as the no-good who had taunted Hector Davis. No decent citizen would play cards at this time of day. All three, Carlsen knew, worked for Mason. Was one of them Mooney? He walked to the table and stood looking down at them. None of the three men looked up from their cards, although they must have known he was standing in front of them.

'Any o' you called Mooney?'

All three looked up. 'You're bustin' up my game,' one said, his grimace showing tobacco-stained teeth. He put his cards on the table before him. 'An' I don't care for it.'

'I'm askin' you agin. Any o' you called Mooney?'

'Mooney ain't here, an' you ain't listenin'!'

With a sweep of his left arm, Carlsen cleared the table of bottle, and glasses, sending cards fluttering to the floor. He lifted his boot and kicked over the table, forcing the men back as their hands dropped to their side-arms. All three froze as they stared down the barrel of Carlsen's Colt.

'Josh saw all three o' you draw first. I kill you all an' no judge is gonna want to know what went on. Put your guns on the floor in front of you, an' do it slowly. Mooney bush-whacked one o' my hands an' he's gonna pay for it. You wanna die for him?'

'OK, take it easy, fer chris'sakes!' the tallest of the three rasped. 'I ain't gonna die lookin' out fer Mooney. We'll do as you say.'

Carlsen stood back a pace, his Colt held high as the three men eased their sidearms from their holsters and bent to place them on the sawdust-covered floor.

'Now kick 'em towards me,' ordered Carlsen, watching their hands. He guessed that all three men had a hidden knife. The guns shifted a couple of feet out of their reach as they did as they were told. 'OK, I ain't standin' here all day,' Carlsen said. 'Where do I find Mooney?'

'You go to—'

Wood chips flew an inch from the speaker's boot as the sound of Carlsen's Colt reverberated around the saloon. The three men jumped back, cursing.

'You got one more chance,' Carlsen barked. 'You tell me where Mooney is or one of you ain't gonna be walkin' for a while.' He looked at each man in turn. 'Which one o' you is that?'

'OK, fer chris'sakes! Mooney's in the corral at the end o' the street. Lookin' after his horse or somethin'.'

'He'd better be there or I'll be back,' rasped Carlsen.

'Now you all turn around an' walk to the end o' the saloon.'

Silently, the men turned and without looking back, walked as far as the musicians' platform. Carlsen turned towards the bar.

'I don't like causin' trouble, Josh, but I ain't standin' by when a young feller gets bushwhacked.'

The barkeep said nothing. Instead, he merely nodded and carried on polishing a glass. Carlsen took a couple of paces back before turning and moving smartly through the batwing doors, out on to the boardwalk. A few men clustered on the street in front of the saloon, drawn by the sound of the shot but the expression on Carlsen's face told them it was not the time to be asking questions. Carlsen pushed through them, unhitched his horse, and trotted his mount down Main Street.

Reaching the corral, Carlsen swung down from his saddle, hooked the reins of his horse over a rail and pushed open the gate. He stood for a moment, watching. In the corral, a tall, lean man was inspecting the foreleg plate of a horse hitched to a rail.

'Your name Mooney?' Carlsen called.

Maybe there was a note in his voice that prompted the tall man to drop the horse's leg, and turn slowly in Carlsen's direction.

'Who's askin'?'

'I ain't gonna ask agin. Your name Mooney?'

'What if it is? What's it to you, cowboy?'

'Young hand o' mine got bushwhacked. You shoulda got that plate fixed. Charlie found your tracks, an' I seen 'em.'

'You callin' me a bushwhacker?' Mooney's hand moved to hover above the butt of his sidearm. 'You could get yourself killed goin' round shootin' your mouth off like that.'

'I ain't aimin' for any killin'. Sheriff Fenner can hear what I gotta say. You can answer to him.'

Instead of replying, Mooney moved away from his horse and edged his way to the centre of the corral. Carlsen didn't move. He was maybe ten yards from Mooney. Not many men could shoot accurately with a heavy sidearm at that distance. Even if Mooney beat him to the draw, he knew his chances were good that he'd be the last man standing.

'Mooney, the doc reckons the kid will make it. You ain't facin' a charge o' killin'.'

'I ain't facin' no charge!' Mooney's hand dropped to the butt of his sidearm.

Carlsen turned his body side-on to Mooney as he heard the hiss of the slug from Mooney's sidearm pass a foot away and slam into a bar of the corral. He raised his Colt, his arm bar-rigid, fully extended. As a second slug whipped past him and splinters again flew from the rails behind him, he squeezed the trigger. A red stain splattered across Mooney's face and he pitched forward, face down in the dirt. Carlsen lowered his arm, holding his Colt at his side, his eyes never leaving Mooney. He walked slowly to the body, checking that Mooney was dead. For a few seconds, he stared at the unseeing open eyes. Then he spat into the dirt.

'Goddamnit!'

Behind him he heard the pounding of feet as the townsfolk hurried to find out what was going on. His mouth set as he knew Fenner would not be far behind. Sure enough, the sheriff's voice rang out above the excited chattering of the men and women.

'Hold it there, Jack! Deputy's got a long gun on you. Put your Colt on the ground an' step away.'

Carlsen did as he was ordered. He didn't think Fenner would give the order to shoot him but if he was to walk away from this he'd be crazy to rile the sheriff. He bent to place the Colt in the soft soil of the corral, stood up, and turned slowly to face Fenner and the crowd of townsfolk.

'Mooney bushwhacked one o' my hands, jest a young feller, Frank. I was tryin' to bring Mooney to you.'

Fenner said something Carlsen didn't catch, and carrying the long gun, the deputy unhitched the gate of the corral and moved to pick up Carlsen's Colt.

'Sheriff wants you to walk across to him,' he said.

Again Carlsen did as he was ordered, conscious of the stares from the townsfolk who fell back a pace or two as he skirted the corral fence.

'Like old times,' he said to Fenner.

The sheriff didn't smile. 'Walk your horse down to my office. You make a run for it an' I'll shoot you down.'

'Aw, c'mon, Frank. You've known me fer ten years. I ain't some no-good gunslinger shootin' up Main Street.'

'Jest do as I'm tellin' you,' Fenner said. 'Gimme that Navy Colt,' he called to his deputy, 'An' then shift what's left o' that no-good.' He turned back to Carlsen. 'I tol' you once. Get on your horse an' take it easy back to the jailhouse.'

He stood watching as Carlsen went across to his palomino and swung into the saddle. The crowd parted to let both horses through, with Fenner riding a few paces behind Carlsen. Together they walked their horses down Main Street, townsfolk keeping up with them. The buzz of conversation showed they were keen to know what was going to happen next.

The two men reined in at the hitching rail in front of Fenner's office. Both stepped down from their saddles. The sheriff turned to the townsfolk as several men ran across the street, attracted by the noise of excited voices.

'OK, folks,' called Fenner. 'Back to your work.'

'You gonna put him in jail?' A shout came from somewhere in the crowd.

'I'm gonna find out what it's all about,' Fenner said. 'I

67

ain't sayin' anymore. Now move off or you're gonna end up in a cage with him.'

He turned and gestured to Carlsen that he should enter the office, stepping behind him and closing the door. He went behind his desk, to lay Carlsen's Colt before him and took his seat.

'Sit down,' Fenner ordered. 'We gotta fill in some paper.'

'What you plannin' on?' Carlsen said, taking the seat in front of the desk.

'I'm plannin' on keepin' you in the jailhouse until Judge Williams arrives next week.'

'Fer chris'sakes! I gotta ranch to look after! Mooney bushwhacked one o' my hands. He drew first. Hell! He had two shots at me before I had to stop him.'

Fenner ignored Carlsen's protest, taking a sheet of paper from the top drawer of his desk. 'You can tell all that to the judge. An' I gotta tell you somethin'. Judge Williams is old enough to remember your name from before you took up ranchin'. He could say you had right on your side, but that's up to him.' He looked up suddenly as the door from the street was flung open. 'See me later, mister, I'm busy.'

'My name is Davis, Sheriff, I am a lawyer and Mr Carlsen is my client. I have a legal right to know what is going on.'

Open-mouthed, Carlsen turned to see Hector Davis standing a few feet inside the door. He appeared to have grown about three inches, and his thumbs were tucked beneath his leather suspenders as though below a silk waist-coat in a courtroom back east.

'Since when we got a new lawyer in town?' Fenner barked.

'Since I arrived with the new owner of the Bar Circle. Do not be misled by the clothes I'm wearing, Mr Fenner. I have one of the largest law firms in New York. One telegraph message and I could have twenty lawyers crawling over every inch of this town. I saw what happened in the corral. Mr Carlsen attempted to bring Mooney to you.'

'I might believe you,' Fenner said. 'But Carlsen's goin' to jail an' the judge will decide.'

Davis stepped forward, and took the seat alongside Carlsen. He leaned towards Fenner, his voice low. 'If you put Mr Carlsen in jail, I shall travel to Cheyenne. I shall see Governor Thayer's senior law officer.' He paused as Fenner gave a dismissive wave of his hand. 'Oh, yes, he'll see me. He'll probably invite me to his home for supper. By the time I've finished, there'll not be a town in the Territory that will have you as a lawman.'

Fenner threw his pen on to his desk, his face red with anger. 'Damn it all! Don't you sonsabitches know all I'm tryin' to do is run a quiet town for decent folks?'

Davis leaned back, his face expressionless. 'Exactly, Mr Fenner. You're doing a fine job and I shall certainly mention it when I'm in Cheyenne.'

Fenner looked at Carlsen, and then he tore up the paper in front of him. 'I ain't sure what you're tryin' to finish, Carlsen. But get it over real quick.'

Davis took a sip of his coffee with the relish of a man tasting fine wine.

'Jack let that brute Mooney take two shots at him,' he said, 'before he was forced to kill him. Then Fenner was going to throw him in jail.'

Carlsen laughed aloud. 'You shoulda seen the sheriff's face when Hector stormed in an' tol' him I had a high-rankin' lawyer from New York.'

If Jane registered any thoughts at both men being on first name terms she didn't show it, save for a slight twitch of one eyebrow.

'We're running a ranch here,' she said dryly. 'We're not

living in a dime novel.'

'But that's the whole point, Jane,' Davis said. 'You can use something like this in one of your books. Think how your readers will appreciate that you're writing about the real West.' He stopped suddenly, looking thoughtful.

'Hector?' Jane said.

'I've just been thinking about Fenner.' Davis turned to Carlsen. 'How often in the Territory would a sheriff throw a man in jail for what you did today?'

Carlsen grimaced. 'You saw what happened in the corral. No other sheriff in Wyoming would have threatened to put me in front of a judge.'

'How honest is Fenner?'

'Far as I know, he's straight. He thinks too much of the town and not enough about the ranches but I guess that's just his way of runnin' the job.'

Davis pursed his lips. 'Maybe with you out of the way, he was making it easier for someone to take over the Bar Circle.'

'But that puts him in cahoots with Hendrix or mebbe even Mason from the saloon.'

'What do you know about him?' Jane asked.

Carlsen shrugged. 'Not much. He was in the army, I think. Came to Jensen about the same time I started to work for Mr Jackson. Got himself elected sheriff eight years ago, an' he's done a good job. Folks are happy to have him wearin' the badge.'

Davis got to his feet. 'I'm going to ride back into town and send a couple of telegraph messages. I'd like to know more about Sheriff Fenner.'

CHAPTER SEVEN

Jane Nicholls stood a few yards from the ranch house with her hands on her hips, her eyes sparkling with anger.

'Mr Carlsen, I'm grateful that you tracked down the man who shot Sean but you're getting above your station! When I give an order to Ethan, I expect it to be obeyed.'

'What did you tell him to do?'

'I gave him instructions to have my horse here an hour after breakfast.'

'An' what did he say?'

'He said he wasn't to give me a horse unless you were here.'

Carlsen nodded. 'Good. That's what I tol' him.'

Jane rapped her whip against her corduroy riding pants. 'I am going into town, Mr Carlsen, where I shall give a talk to the Ladies Society. I am perfectly able to ride to Jensen by myself.'

Carlsen breathed in deeply. A couple of days before, he'd reckoned that he and Jane had finally learned to get along with each other and arguments like these were in the past. Now it seemed he was going to have to start all over again, rebuilding his fences.

'I'll ride in with you,' he said.

'Oh, for pity's sake!'

'I said I'll ride in with you,' he cut in.

'Jack Carlsen! Sometimes!'

Her face was red with frustration, and for a moment Carlsen thought she was about to strike him with her raised whip. Then she brought it down with a loud whack against her leg.

'Have my horse here in ten minutes!'

She turned on her heel and went to step up to the porch.

'Just one moment, ma'am.'

She whirled to face him. 'What is it now?'

'I don't reckon you should go into town wearin' those pants.'

'Why shouldn't I? They are extremely fashionable back east.'

'That's it, ma'am. They're mebbe fine back east but you wear those in Jenson an' folks will be sayin' you're no better than you should be.'

'And what does that mean, Mr Carlsen?'

Carlsen twisted up his mouth. 'They're gonna say you'll be the first ranch owner who's gonna end up workin' in the Silver Dollar.'

To Carlsen's surprise, Jane threw back her head and burst out laughing.

'Honestly, Mr Carlsen, I sometimes wonder what you and the men really think of me.' She smiled. 'And I suppose you want me in a buggy, wearing a broad-brimmed hat with a silk bow.'

'The side-saddle will be fine.'

'Very well,' she said, her eyes twinkling. 'But I'll still ride the chestnut.'

The sun was creeping up in the sky when Jane and Carlsen trotted their horses down Main Street towards the hitching rail outside the town's best hotel. Carlsen was aware that they were creating a stir among the townsfolk of Jensen Flats. Little clusters of men and women on the boardwalks turned to see Jane dressed in her fashionable riding clothes. Half a dozen of the townsfolk called out greetings and Jane acknowledged them with a wave of her gloved hand.

Carlsen felt good about riding through the town with such an attractive young woman, even if she was his boss. He was pleased that Jane had finally recovered her good temper as she looked across at him with a smile.

'Maybe they think you have a wife now, Mr Carlsen.'

'My wife and son died ten years ago from cholera, Miss Jane. I ain't never thought o' bein' hitched agin.'

Jane's smile was wiped from her face. 'I'm sorry. I didn't know that.'

Carlsen shrugged. 'No reason you should.' He reined in as they reached the hotel. 'Here's where you're gonna talk to the ladies.' He swung down from the saddle, and held out his hand for Jane to step down. 'You can tell 'em about the shootin' an' the wild men you've been meetin'.'

'I think they'll want to hear about the latest fashions in hats.' She smiled. 'I'll be two hours. No more.'

'I'll be here, Miss Jane.'

Carlsen watched her step up to the boardwalk and enter the hotel. She was a fine-looking woman, there was no argument with that. What in tarnation had prompted him to mention his late wife and son? Truth be told, save for the fading daguerreotype of the woman he'd married and who'd borne him a son, he could barely remember what she'd looked like.

He finished securing both horses to the hitching rail, feeling for a moment or two a little empty. Living out at the ranch was a fine way of life but sometimes when he visited Jensen, he wondered if there should be more.

He shook his head as if to chase off his thoughts. A beer in the Silver Dollar would set him aright. Mason's no-goods would be no trouble now he'd shown them he could use his Colt, and wouldn't hesitate to do so if the situation demanded it. He crossed the street, already beginning to think of that first taste of beer. He pushed through the batwing doors. A solitary drinker was sitting over by the far wall, his feet on a nearby chair, his hat tipped over his eyes. Josh was wiping down the bar with a cloth.

'Howdy, Mr Carlsen. One beer comin' up.'

'Thanks, Josh. You got the *Clarion*?'

The barkeep bent to reach below the bar, and pulled out the local newspaper, placing it in front of Carlsen.

'A coupla pages on your new boss,' he said. 'Makes real interestin' readin'. She's a famous lady back east.'

Carlsen spread the paper on the bar and turned the pages until he reached the large black letters announcing that JB Nicholls was in Jensen and would be talking to the Ladies Society. Carlsen read on. That morning she'd learned something new about him. Maybe the newspaper would tell him something new about her. Then he froze as he felt the pressure against the small of his back. A hoarse voice whispered in his ear.

'You go for that Colt, Carlsen, an' you're a dead man.'

Carlsen looked at the mirror behind the bar but whoever it was behind him had positioned himself to have Carlsen's reflection covering his face.

'What the hell you want?'

The hoarse voice was close to his ear. 'I'll settle for a glass of sarsaparilla!'

A face suddenly appeared in the mirror alongside Carlsen's, bearing a large grin. 'Got you there, Jack!'

Carlsen whirled around, recognizing the speaker imme-diately. 'Fer chris'sakes, Hank Mather!' He flung an arm around the other's shoulder while grasping Mather by the hand and shaking it vigorously. 'How long's it been? Ten years, mebbe twelve?'

'Twelve years since Green Valley an' that damned sheriff who nearly got us both killed.'

'Josh! A beer for Mr Mather.' Carlsen turned back from the bar. 'You still keepin' to the rule?'

'Sure am. No whiskey afore nightfall. Kept us both alive so far.'

Carlsen picked up the beer and handed it to Mather. 'I was takin' a beer while hangin' 'round for my boss.'

'Your boss? What you doin' nowadays?'

'I'm ranchin'. Got to bein' range boss now.'

Mather's jaw dropped. 'Range boss? You mean handlin' cattle an' brandin' an' stuff like that?'

Carlsen grinned. 'Yeah, stuff like that. Been doin' it since we got into that barrel o' tar in Green Valley. Jackson Nicholls took me on an' I've been at the Bar Circle ever since.' His grin widened at the other's expression. 'Bet you never thought I'd do it.'

'No, I never did,' Mather said slowly. 'When you said you were quittin' I reckoned it was on account o' what happened.' He looked hard at Carlsen. 'You cain't blame yourself, Jack. That damn sheriff was the one who caused it.'

'That was enough gun fightin' for me,' Carlsen said. 'Anyways, I enjoy punchin' cattle. The Bar Circle's been through rough times but now we got a feisty young gal as the new owner an' I reckon we'll pull through.' He saw Mather's expression harden and he frowned. 'What's wrong?'

Mather breathed in deeply. 'The Bar Circle's why I'm here. I got hired in Cheyenne by some critter who said he was actin' for his boss in Jensen Flats. He promised me enough to fill my poke an' tol' me the job was easy. No

75

killin', just scare off folks.'

Carlsen took a long look at his old partner. 'How long you just been scarin' off folks, Hank?' he asked quietly.

'Now don't you start preachin' at me!' Mather said sharply. 'Ten years ago, things were different. It ain't so easy to get a livin' nowadays, doin' what we do.'

'I don't anymore,' Carlsen said. He took an inch off his beer. 'You gonna tell me who's hired you?'

Mather shook his head. 'I cain't. I was tol' to ride here an' wait. Some feller would come an' talk to me.'

'You gonna tell me when you find out?'

'Fer chris'sakes, Jack. We ain't gonna end up fightin' each other but I gotta get my hands on some money or I'm gonna be just another saddle-bum, driftin' around.'

Carlsen finished his beer and stood up. 'You think about it, Hank. I'll see you around. We'll get together an' drink too much whiskey. Right now I got business with a coupla stores.'

Carlsen walked along the boards fronting the stores along Main Street, turning over in his mind his meeting with his old partner. He'd made the right decision ten years before to take the job with old Jackson Nicholls and put down his gun. Sure, his Colt was now back on his hip but it wouldn't be there for long. Hendrix would soon realize that he wasn't getting his hands on the Bar Circle. Jane Nicholls would bring in money from back east and the two ranches would get back to equal standing. Hendrix would back off and life would get back to normal.

Carlsen still couldn't accept that the old rancher was behind the shooting of Sean. Hendrix was a ruthless, land-hungry son of a bitch but he wasn't a bushwhacker, or likely to hire one. So was Mason behind all the efforts to scare off Jane Nicholls? Maybe the saloon-owner and his bunch of no-goods were being used by someone else.

He passed the hotel and checked Jane's horse and his own, both of which were standing half asleep at the hitching rail. His pace quickened as he realized he had a little more than an hour to carry out his chores before he had to return to collect Jane and accompany her back to the Bar Circle.

An hour later he was walking back to the hotel, clutching a package he'd picked up in the dry goods store. Hector Davis had told him that he could be eating supper in the Big House and he reckoned a couple of new shirts wouldn't go amiss. Then he saw Eliza Parsons approaching him along the boardwalk. That meant Jane had finished her talk and the ladies were leaving.

'Howdy, Eliza. Guess I should hurry along. Miss Jane's waiting for me. I hope her talk went well.'

The attractive widow looked puzzled. 'Our group don't meet this week, Jack. I'm yet to write to Miss Nicholls to arrange a date.'

It was Carlsen's turn to look puzzled. 'Must be a misunderstandin'.' He touched the brim of his hat. 'I'd best be goin'.'

Five minutes later Carlsen walked into the hotel, and looked around the chairs and leather-covered chesterfields placed around the area in front of the desk. He went across to the clerk who had his head down, examining the pages of a large book.

'I'm lookin' fer Miss Jane Nicholls, owner of the Bar Circle. She came in a coupla hours ago.'

'I'm not sure I know the lady.'

'Young, fancy hat, smart ridin' clothes. Her horse is on the rail with mine.'

Again the clerk shook his head. 'There's a meeting in the large parlour but they're all men. You could try the small parlour. Along the passageway to your right.'

Carlsen turned on his heel and strode across the hotel to enter the passageway. The door to the small parlour was ajar and he pushed it open to find that the room was empty. He turned around to return to the clerk and saw one of the hotel maids standing a few feet away.

'I heard you talkin' at the desk,' she said. 'I saw the lady.'

'When was that?'

'When she came into the hotel. A gentleman who'd been waiting stood up and spoke with her. Then they walked along here.'

'Did you see her after that?'

The maid shook her head. 'I thought she'd left because the door was open.

'I had to shut it.' She pointed past Carlsen to the end of the corridor. 'Ladies and gentlemen don't often use that door as it opens on to an alleyway.'

Carlsen felt the muscles across his gut clench. Was he jumping to crazy notions? She could have met someone she knew and stepped out for a while. But where would she have gone? If she'd decided to take coffee with a friend, she would surely have taken it here in the hotel. He'd been up and down Main Street during the past hour or so, and there'd been no sign of her.

He nodded his thanks to the maid, and turned to stride to the end of the hallway and push open the door. The maid was right. The alleyway was not a place where folks in smart clothes would choose to step. In the shadows, the dirt was still drying out from the winter snow and Carlsen caught the acrid smell of rotting vegetation. There were footprints and cart tracks but they could have been made by anyone in the last day or so. He was about to step back into the passageway

78

when he caught sight of something small and shiny caught on a spindly plant. Out of curiosity, he stepped across the mud and bent to pull it clear. It was a thin bracelet. Letters were engraved on the small silver plate. He didn't need to read them. He'd noticed the bracelet on Jane's wrist that morning.

He breathed in deeply, strode down the alleyway and around the corner of the hotel on to Main Street. A couple of minutes later, he was pushing through the batwing doors of the Silver Dollar. A few men lined the bar, but against the wall, his feet on the rungs of a chair on the other side of the table, Mather sat nursing his beer. He looked up as Carlsen approached him and frowned at his old partner's expression.

'Somethin' wrong, Jack?'

'Some sonovabitch has made away with my boss. She's a lovely lady, a gentlewoman. Christ knows what they'll do to her. There's a bunk in my cabin back at the ranch, you'll get food, an' I'll buy your ammunition. Davis at the ranch might find you some money.'

Mather looked at him for several seconds. Then he finished his beer and stood up. 'Aw, hell! I can always go work in a store. You'll haveta find me a better horse.'

An hour later, the two men reined in on the outskirts of town. Mather sat astride a big grey horse, loaned to him from the livery. Both men had saddlebags with spare ammunition, water, and pemmican.

'They've got mebbe two or three hours on us,' Carlsen said. 'Ride to nightfall and then at dawn ride to the Bar Circle. I'll meet you there.' He stared hard at Mather. 'You catch up with 'em, you kill 'em.'

'S'posin' Miss Jane's unharmed?'

'You kill 'em, anyways.' Carlsen turned his horse's head. 'I'm gamblin' they've gone either north or south. You keep goin' north an' you'll come across a sheepman. He coulda seen somethin'.'

Mather touched the brim of his hat. 'I'll be seein' you, Jack.'

Carlsen rode steadily south for an hour. Nothing stirred across the flat lands of bunch and buffalo grass ahead of him, save for a couple of jack-rabbits as big as cattle dogs. Once clear of Jensen, he'd spent a couple of minutes trying to pick up tracks, but the trail had been used too often at the beginning of spring to offer any chance of tracking a wagon or a bunch of horses.

He reckoned he'd been riding for another hour when he saw the first signs of life ahead of him. Two men astride their horses riding his way heading, he guessed, for Jensen Flats. Maybe they'd seen something. He was about a couple of hundred yards from the men when he reined in and held up a hand.

'Howdy, I need your help if you got time to spare.'

The two men looked at each other, one of them resting his hand on the butt of the pistol at his waist. Carlsen kept both of his hands where the two men could see them. The riders slowed their mounts to a walk and walked their horses to close Carlsen. One of them spoke.

'You the range boss out at the Bar Circle? I seen you afore.'

'That's it, Carlsen's the name.' He thought quickly. No sense in the whole of Jensen knowing what was going on. 'I'm tryin' to catch up with some folks, mebbe a coupla hours ahead o' me. You seen anyone?'

'Yeah, reckon we have. Mebbe an hour or so back.'

'What these folks look like?'

'Three riders, an' a feller drivin' a wagon. There was someone in the back o' the wagon, but we couldn't see much.'

'They say anythin'?'

'Nope. We wished 'em good day but they weren't of a mind fer talkin'.'

'Thanks, boys. You ever out at the Bar Circle, you come in an' get coffee.'

'We'll do that.'

Carlsen dug his heels into the sides of his roan. If Jane was in the wagon there was every chance she was still alive, otherwise the likelihood was that her body would have been hidden where it would never be found. Who were these men who had taken her? In the days before he'd taken up ranching, men riding the owl hoot trail kept women out of their business. Even the calico queens in the saloons weren't treated badly, and no man would manhandle a gentlewoman or be coarse in her company. Maybe the railroad was bringing to the west a harsher and more ruthless no-good.

He rode for almost another hour. If he didn't find anything before nightfall, he knew he could only return to the Bar Circle at dawn, after sleeping beneath the stars. Then he'd plan what to do next. He was thinking about the odds of Mather having success on the trail to the north, when he shouted out loudly in triumph.

Maybe five miles ahead of him, he could just make out the dark patches of what he guessed was the wagon and riders described by the two cowboys. He urged his mount forwards, the horse blowing air through his nostrils, the animal's ears flicking backwards and forwards as the Plains spurs nicked his sides.

Carlsen unsheathed his Winchester, his eyes fixed on the wagon which kept on rolling at a steady speed. Had they not heard him? The speed of his horse brought him closer to the wagon and he hitched the reins around the horn of his saddle and levered the long gun. Aiming above the heads of the three riders, he pulled the trigger.

The wagon came to an abrupt halt, the three riders turning their horses to face Carlsen as he rode forwards, the Winchester moving back and forth covering the four men.

'What the hell you do that for?'

The speaker was the heavy-set man driving the wagon, who looked as if he'd led a hard life, his face marked with deep lines of ingrained tiredness. The three riders were young men, dressed from head to foot in black, silver glinting from their belt buckles and their spurs.

'All three of you get off your horses. You stay where you are,' Carlsen ordered the driver.

'We ain't got anythin' worth your stealin,' said one of the younger men.

'Shut your mouth,' Carlsen barked.

Without taking his eyes off the four men he stepped down from his saddle, his long gun in hand, and edged to stand alongside the wagon. Over the board he saw the outline of a figure wrapped in white cotton. Was Jane dead or only unconscious?

'Come here,' Carlsen ordered the younger of the men who had spoken. 'Unwrap that cotton sheet.'

'I cain't do that!'

His long gun in his left hand, Carlsen drew his Colt and cocked it. 'Do it!'

Ashen-faced, his eyes wide with fear, the young man put one foot on the spoke of the wagon wheel and boosted himself on to the bed of the wagon. He knelt on one knee and slowly unwound the end of the sheet. Carlsen was able to see a woman's face. For a moment he was unable to breathe. He felt as if he'd been kicked by a mustang. He turned to the older man.

'Christ, I'm sorry! My boss, a gentlewoman got taken and I thought—'

'Save it, mister! That's my wife o' thirty years an' these boys' mother, an' we're takin' her home to be laid to rest. Now get the hell outta my sight!'

CHAPTER EIGHT

Hector Davis, clad in work clothes, stood at the entrance to the horse-barn with a long-handled hayfork in his hands. Wisps of straw brushed at his shoulders and sweat was running down the side of his face. He looked across the yard as Carlsen walked his mount towards him.

'Where the hell have you been, Jack?' he called. 'We were damned worried last night. And where's JB?'

'You seen a feller by the name o' Mather?' Carlsen asked, ignoring the question, as he stepped down from his saddle.

'No, I haven't,' snapped Davis. 'Are you going to answer my question?'

'Miss Jane's been taken away by no-goods. Me and my partner's been out lookin'.'

'Oh, my god!' Davis's face was chalk-white. 'Have you told the sheriff?'

Carlsen shook his head. 'No time. I wanted to get back here to meet up with my partner. He went north, I went south,' he added as explanation. 'He coulda caught up with 'em.'

'I don't reckon so,' Davis said harshly. He took a hand from the pole to point over Carlsen's shoulder. 'That could be your partner now.'

Carlsen turned to see Mather riding towards them. He

was alone, and as he drew closer, Carlsen could see his face was grim. Obviously, he'd fared no better than Carlsen himself.

Mather stepped down from his horse. He looked at Carlsen and shook his head. 'You wanna put my horse in the barn,' he said to Davis. 'I haveta speak to Mr Carlsen.'

'Hold on, Hank,' Carlsen cut in. 'This is Mr Hector Davis. He works for Miss Jane.'

Davis turned back to the barn. 'Billy,' he called. A boy Carlsen hadn't seen before appeared at the doorway to the barn and Davis turned to Mather. 'Billy will take care of your horse. Ethan's ridden up to the beef with stuff for the chuck wagon. You two men follow me. We've some thinking to do.'

As Billy led away Mather's horse, Davis strode purposefully towards the house, leaving Carlsen and Mather looking at each other.

'He sure knows how to give an order fer a feller pushin' hay in a barn,' Mather said.

Two minutes later, the three men were seated in the parlour. Mugs of coffee were in their hands, having been brought to them by Lucy. Carlsen could see she was bursting to ask questions but he saw no advantage in upsetting her and Mrs Gittins. He'd need to tell the new boy in the horse-barn to keep his mouth shut if he'd heard any of the brief conversation with Hector Davis.

'Tell me what went on,' Davis said to Carlsen.

Briefly, Carlsen told him of riding into Jensen, leaving Miss Jane at the hotel entrance and returning a couple of hours later to find that she'd disappeared. Mather, his old partner, had agreed to help find Miss Jane.

Davis thought for a moment. 'Will they kill her?'

'Jesus, Hector!' Carlsen said sharply. The bluntness of the lawyer's mind took him aback. But it was inevitable that Davis, no doubt thinking of the future, would ask the question. He thought for a moment. 'Miss Jane said once you handled all her business affairs.'

Davis nodded. 'That's correct.'

'Could you sign to sell the Bar Circle?'

Davis pulled his lips hard against his teeth. 'Yes, I could. You think that's what they're planning?'

'I read in the *Clarion* Miss Jane moves among powerful folks. They know you'll not risk everything she has back east. Mebbe they're plannin' that Hendrix moves in an' buys the ranch afore they let her go unharmed.'

'This Hendrix some sorta owl hoot?' Mather asked.

'He's a big-time rancher, owns the Lazy Y spread.' Carlsen chewed his lip. 'That's why all this is crazy. Hendrix's a sonovabitch but he ain't likely to go takin' a gentlewoman like Miss Jane or hirin' men to do it for him.'

'You think it could be his son?' Hector said.

Carlsen nodded. 'Grant Hendrix might just do things his pa knows nothing about. He lied to his pa about gettin' rid o' the nesters.'

'Whatever you decide, you must remember that I can't take a chance with JB's well-being,' Davis said flatly.

'I know that,' Carlsen said. 'So we gotta find her an' bring her home.'

'But where do we start looking?' Davis said gloomily.

The three men looked to the door as a feverish knocking sounded.

'Come!' Davis called.

Lucy stood at the door. 'Ethan's at the door. He's actin' like a scalded cat.'

'Send him in,' Davis ordered.

A moment later Ethan stood at the doorway, 'Mr Davis, sir. I was comin' back from takin' stuff up to the beef an' I took a quick ride to take a look at our old shanty. I saw Miss Jane with some men. She was in a buggy.' He swallowed hard a couple of times. 'But her hands were tied, Mr Davis. She was a prisoner, I swear it! She was struggling but they pushed her into the shanty.'

The three men jumped to their feet.

'I want two fresh horses outside, saddled and ready to go in five minutes, Ethan. Go!' Carlsen ordered. He turned to Davis and held up a hand. 'I ain't riskin' you, Hector. You're too important for Miss Jane. You're stayin' here.'

'But—' Hector began to protest.

'We'll bring her back, Hector.'

Without waiting for Davis's reply, he swung on his heel and strode out of the room, closely followed by Mather.

Carlsen and Mather had reached the stand of cottonwoods on foot, maybe 200 yards from the old Ford shanty. Their horses had been tethered away far enough for the animals not to catch the scent of the three horses tied to the rail a few feet from the shanty's door. One of the horses was without a saddle. At the corner of the shanty stood a buggy, its horseless shafts resting on the ground.

'You see any of 'em?' Carlsen said softly.

'Nothin's movin',' Mather said, his voice low. 'You reckon there's three of 'em?'

'I reckon so. Two riders an' one fer the buggy.' He raised his Winchester. 'One way to find out, I guess.'

He raised the barrel of the 1873 Winchester long gun until he was aiming for the roof of the shanty, his finger hooked around the trigger and he let off a shot. In the still air of the early summer, the slug sounded around the trees and the higher ground beyond the shanty, hitting the dirt roof with a solid thud. From the inside of the shanty came raised voices.

Carlsen nodded grimly. 'Three it is.' He lowered the Winchester and leaned it against the trunk of a cottonwood.

Cupping his hands around his mouth, he called out, 'You in the shanty. You hear me?'

There was silence for a few seconds then a hoarse voice called out. 'We hear you. You shoot agin an' we're gonna kill the gel.'

Carlsen breathed in deeply. 'You lay a finger on her an' all three of you are gonna die. An' it's gonna be slow.'

'How do we know Miss Nicholls is still alive?' Mather said tersely. 'They could be bluffin'.'

Carlsen nodded. Again he cupped his hands to call out. 'I wanna hear the woman.'

There was no reply from the shanty. The seconds ticked over and still nothing stirred. Carlsen felt as if a band of iron was across his chest. If the men in the shanty had harmed Jane, he'd make sure they suffered before they died.

'Mr Carlsen, I'm here!'

It was Jane's voice. She sounded unharmed, her voice clear.

'Be brave, Miss Jane,' he called. 'We'll soon have you home.'

The sounds of a scuffle came from the shanty as if something had been knocked over. Carlsen heard a stifled shout of anger, and then a voice rang out.

'Your play, Carlsen! Or whateva your name is!'

'There's two of us out here. We got half a dozen men comin' up with us. Let the woman go an' you three can ride outta here.'

'You crazy? We let her go an' you'll shoot us down.'

Carlsen swallowed a couple of times. If Jane Nicholls was to come out of this unharmed, he'd need to take a chance. If shooting started there was always the risk of her being hit.

'OK, tell you what we'll do. I'll walk to you unarmed?'

'Are you crazy?' Mather barked.

Carlsen ignored him. 'I'll walk to you unarmed,' he

called again. 'You ride out an' that way we all get to live.'

'Your partner could still shoot us down.'

'I'll not do that,' Mather called. 'I give you my range word. But you trick my partner an' I'll kill the three o' you, woman or not.'

Carlsen heard the three men talking, and then the voice of the no-good Carlsen guessed was their leader rang out across the open ground. 'OK! You come out from behind those trees. I don't wanna see any iron about you.'

'I hope to hell you know what you're doin',' Mather said.

His mouth set, Carlsen unbuckled his gun belt and allowed it to fall to the ground behind him. He stepped away from the protection of the cottonwood until he was clear of the trees and standing on the open ground. He stood motionless, aware that he was beginning to sweat. The no-goods could still try to shoot him down and then take their chances against Mather. They'd be signing their own death warrants. He'd seen Mather in action many times when they'd worked together. But how would Jane fare?

There was a movement from the side of the shanty as a board was pushed open a few inches and Carlsen could see the outline of a man holding a long gun, the barrel aimed at him. He took a step forwards, holding his hands away from his body.

'Keep walkin' an' I wanna see those hands all the time!'

Step by step, Carlsen covered the ground. He could see that if the no-good attempted to shoot, he would have to push open the board and he'd be exposed.

Mather wouldn't miss from this range and there'd be a few precious seconds to make it back to the shelter of the trees. He could feel the sweat beneath the band of his Stetson begin to trickle down the side of his face. Was the day that warm?

After what seemed like a very long time, he was four or

five yards from the door of the shanty, his hands still away from his sides. In front of him the door was slowly inched back.

'No tricks,' Carlsen said tersely.

Slowly, the door opened to reveal a tall swarthy man, his beard long enough to touch the front of his rough blue shirt. In his hand he held an 1860 army revolver with the eight-inch barrel. He raised it to aim directly at Carlsen.

'Who hired you?' Carlsen said.

His question was ignored. Apparently satisfied that Carlsen was unarmed, the man turned to look back into the shanty. 'OK, we're outta here. We ain't signed on to get ourselves shot up.'

Carlsen took a pace back as the three men came out of the shanty, one of them carrying a saddle which he threw over the horse that must have been used to haul the buggy. Nobody spoke while he secured the saddle before turning and nodding that all was ready. The three men stepped up to their saddles, the leader turning in his saddle to look down at Carlsen.

'Your partner in the trees. His name Mather, by any chance?'

Carlsen nodded.

'Didn't know you two were still in the Territory. You ain't gonna hold this agin me, are you?'

'You gonna tell me who hired you?'

'Guess it don't matter anymore. Feller by the name o' Laker.'

Laker? Who the hell was Laker?

'I see you 'round these parts agin,' Carlsen said, 'I'm gonna kill you.'

'Yeah, guess you'd say that. Anyways, we wuz heading home to Colorado. Seems a fine notion to keep going.' He held up his hand as if bidding farewell to an old friend and turned his mount's head.

Carlsen watched the three men ride away. When he was satisfied they weren't coming back, he turned to signal in the direction of Mather, who was standing in front of the trees facing the retreating riders, his long gun at his shoulder. Carlsen turned towards the shanty. Jane Nicholls, ashen-faced, save for a red mark on her cheek where Carlsen guessed she'd been slapped, stood in the doorway. Her smart riding outfit was streaked with mud, her jacket torn.

As Carlsen moved towards her, she stumbled against him in a swoon. He threw his arms around her, preventing her falling to the ground. For a few moments they stood like statues, her head against his chest. Then her eyes opened and she looked up at him, forcing a weak smile.

'I knew you'd come, Mr Carlsen.'

The determined look on her face collapsed and she began to sob, her head down, tears running down her cheeks and falling to the front of his leather vest. He took his arms from around her and gently held her by her upper arms.

'It's OK now, Miss Jane,' Carlsen said, his voice soft. 'The men have gone an' you're safe.'

'I was frightened they'd—'

'Now don't you think about those things, Miss Jane. You're safe now with me an' Hank. You can ride up with me to the ranch an' we'll have you back with Hector in no time at all.'

Through her tears, Carlsen thought he detected the glimmer of a genuine smile. 'Are all range bosses as brave as you, Mr Carlsen?'

'There's lots braver, Miss Jane.' He grinned. 'I even saw one dance with the mayor's wife.'

If Carlsen's jest had meant to lighten the atmosphere, it

91

misfired badly. Jane pulled away from him, tottered a couple of short steps and would have fallen had Carlsen not been quick to support her.

'I'm so foolish,' he heard her mutter.

'You've bin through a lot, Miss Jane. You ain't foolish at all, you're a brave gal. Now I want you to put your arms around my neck.'

She turned to look up at him, her eyes widening.

'Miss Jane, I ain't askin' anythin' that ain't proper but I gotta carry you someways to my horse, an' you gotta help me.'

For a second, he caught the scent of fresh flowers as he bunched his muscles and lifted her in his arms, her arms around his neck.

Carlsen and Mather were drinking coffee when Hector Davis entered the room.

'JB will be down shortly.'

'How is she?' Carlsen asked.

'She's fine, thanks to you both. You both did a great job.' Davis took his seat and looked across the room. 'You got money in a bank anywhere, Mr Mather?'

Mather frowned. 'I got a few dollars in a bank down in Cheyenne.'

'Give me the details later. I'll arrange a payment of five hundred dollars.'

Mather's jaw dropped. 'Five hundred?'

'Worth every cent,' Davis cut in. 'I hate to think what I'd have been paying for Pinkertons. What's important is that you got JB back safe and sound.'

Mather looked around at Carlsen but before either man could speak, the door opened and Jane Nicholls entered the room.

'Gentlemen,' she acknowledged as the three men got to

their feet. She crossed the room to take her usual soft-backed chair and looked at each one in turn as they took their seats.

'I want to thank you all,' she said.

'Good to see you looking well, Miss Jane,' Carlsen said.

'JB, if we're to find out who hired these vicious men who took you away, we have to ask you some questions,' Davis said. 'I hope it's not too soon.'

She shook her head. 'Ask away, Hector,' she said. 'I feel fine now.'

'Why did you think you had an engagement with the Ladies Society?'

'A letter was delivered here one day last week when you and Mr Carlsen were away.'

'Did you see who delivered the letter?'

'Sheriff Fenner. I offered him coffee but he was keen to be on his way.'

There was silence in the room for a few moments.

'What happened when you entered the hotel?' Carlsen asked.

'I was met by a respectable-looking man, smartly dressed, who explained he would show me to the small parlour at the end of the hall where the ladies were waiting for me. I accompanied him and at the end of the hall, the door to an alley opened. Two men appeared and bundled me into a buggy. One of them held a cloth over my face and I don't remember anything until the buggy was clear of the town.'

'Chloroform,' said Davis flatly.

'What's that you said?' Mather asked.

'Chloroform. It's a new drug used by doctors,' Jane replied. 'It reduces pain by rendering the patient unconscious.'

'The man who met you at the hotel,' Carlsen said. 'Had you seen him before?'

93

Jane shook her head. 'No. He gave the appearance of being a gentleman but there was nothing special about him.' She paused as if recalling something. 'He took off his hat when he met me. I noticed he had a silver streak in his dark hair.'

Hector Davis shot up in his chair as if stung. 'I've seen that man.'

Three pairs of eyes stared hard at him. 'I was in the General Store speaking with Mr Rudman while we were checking the ranch books,' Davis said. 'Two men came into the store. Two ladies entered the store behind them and both took off their hats to greet the ladies. One of the men had black hair with a silver streak, I'm sure of it.'

'Would you know him agin?' Mather asked.

Davis hesitated. 'Only if I saw him hatless.'

'How about the other man?'

'I've seen him before around the town. I think he owns the saloon. Mason, is that his name?'

Carlsen looked at Mather. 'Get your horse, Hank. We're ridin' into Jensen.'

The Silver Dollar appeared to be empty save for the barkeep and a young woman, one of the calico queens, sitting at a table, when Carlsen and Mather pushed through the batwing doors and entered the saloon. They were ten feet from the entrance before Carlsen saw a red-haired man sitting on the stairs leading up to Mason's office and private rooms. He stood up as Carlsen and Mather approached him.

'No goin' up here, gents. Doxie'll get you a drink.'

Without warning, Mather slammed the butt of his sidearm against the red-haired man's neck, sending him crashing backwards on to the stairs.

'You reach for that pistol and my friend here's gonna kill

94

you,' said Carlsen. He stepped forwards. 'Now get outta my way.'

He went up the stairs to Mason's office and pushed open the door. Then he burst out laughing. On the chaise-longue against the wall Mason, his pants off, wearing only pale grey long johns was straddled across a young woman whose face was turned to Carlsen, her eyes wide with surprise.

'Get out! Get outta here, you sonovabitch!' Mason, his face purple with rage, his eyes bulging, pushed himself up on his elbows.

A wide grin on his face, Carlsen pulled a chair from beside the desk, spun it on one of its legs, and leaned on its back. 'Get your pants on, Mason. We gotta talk.' He tilted his head to look at the young woman. 'You wanna push down your skirts, missy, an' get outta here.'

Swearing loudly, Mason pushed himself off the girl, allowing her to struggle to sit up, and pull down her cheap cotton skirt. Carlsen stood up, his hand on the butt of his Colt as Mason pulled on his pants.

'My partner's on the stairs,' he said as the girl scurried past him. 'Don't try anythin' foolish.'

Wordlessly, the girl shook her head and hurried out of the room, closing the door behind her.

'You're gonna pay for this, Carlsen. I've never—'

'Fer chris'sakes, Mason! Stop bellyaching,' Carlsen cut in. 'You tell me what I need to know an' I don't give a damn if you bed every calico queen in the Territory.'

Tucking his shirt into his pants, Mason took his chair behind the desk.

'I ain't gonna tell you anythin',' he snarled. 'You bustin' in here like an animal!'

Carlsen looked at him for a couple of seconds. Then his hand slipped beneath his trail jacket and he brought out his pocket pistol. 'Which one?' he asked.

'What the hell you talkin' about?' Mason said, his eyes on the pistol.

'I'm gonna shoot off one of your ears,' Carlsen said evenly. 'I ain't made up my mind which one.'

Mason snatched at the drawer at the side of his desk, only to freeze as the .22 slug smashed into one of the glass chimneys of the oil-lamp two feet from Mason's head.

'You crazy bastard!' Mason shouted, jerking his hand back from the drawer.

'You gonna talk?'

'OK, OK! What is it you want?'

'You were in the General Store with a stranger coupla days back. Who was he?'

'Fer chris'sakes, Carlsen. I'm in an' outta the store six times a day. How the hell do you expect me to remember?'

'He was tall with a white streak in his black hair.'

Carlsen saw the light of recognition show in Mason's eyes and waited for him to lie.

'Don't mean anythin' to me.'

The remaining glass chimney of the oil lamp shattered, sending fragments of glass across Mason's desk. Carlsen raised his pistol, aiming it directly at Mason.

'The right ear, I reckon.'

'I know who you mean,' Mason said quickly. 'Put that goddamn pistol away. His name's Laker, or anyways that's the name he's usin' now.' Mason's mouth twisted. 'Feller's had half a dozen names since I've known him.'

'Where do I find him?'

Mason shook his head. 'You're too late. He left on the stage coupla hours ago.'

Carlsen jumped to his feet. 'I find you got a hand in this business, I'm comin' back.'

'What business?' Mason asked, but he was talking to an empty room.

CHAPTER NINE

Carlsen came over the brow of the hill, his palomino snorting loudly, the animal's breath clouding the air around its head. Maybe 500 yards ahead, Carlsen could see the stagecoach alongside the corral holding the change horses of the stage station. Carlsen leaned forward and pulled at one of his mount's ears.

'You've done just fine,' he said aloud.

He touched his spurs to the animal's sides. In a few minutes, he'd be confronting Laker and the son of a bitch would talk. He'd make sure of that. Laker would tell him who was behind the taking of Miss Jane. Old man Hendrix surely had to be the one who'd paid Laker but Fenner would need to hear more than accusations.

As he approached the stage he saw two men he recognized. The stage driver and his shotgun were often seen about town. A couple of times when he'd been in the saloon, he'd played cards with them. When he got closer, he saw they were working on one of the Concord's wheels.

'Howdy, Frenchie, Matt,' he greeted them. 'You gotta problem?'

The driver turned. 'Howdy, Mr Carlsen. No big deal. Matt thought one of the wheels was workin' loose. We was just checkin'.'

'I got business with one o' the passengers. They in the station house?'

'Yeah, Bill's rustled up some coffee. We ain't due to stop here, but reckoned we oughta take a look at the wheel.'

'How many passengers you got?'

'Four men. Three strangers an' a soldier boy.'

'Guess I'll get some of that coffee.'

Carlsen turned his mount's head, and walked the animal over to the hitching rail set a few feet from the stationhouse. He stepped down from the saddle, and pushed open the door. Inside the long open room, four men stood around a table. Two wore range clothes, one wore a smart city suit, and a few paces from the group a tall soldier, his blue uniform neatly pressed, stood holding a mug. All four men wore hats. They looked across at Carlsen, mild curiosity showing in their eyes. Carlsen raised a hand in greeting as the station-keeper came through a door, carrying a metal pot.

'Howdy, Mr Carlsen. What brings you to these parts?'

'I got business here, Bill.'

'What sorta business?'

Carlsen drew his Colt, holding the sidearm loose by his side. 'This kinda business.'

'What the hell?'

'You three men,' Carlsen ordered, 'over by the wall. Soldier boy, you stay where you are.'

One of the men stepped forward. 'I don't take orders—'

'Then you're the one I'm lookin' fer.' Carlsen thumbed back the hammer of his Colt.

'OK! Take it easy!'

The three men shuffled away from the table until their backs were against the wall. Pale-faced, they stared back at Carlsen. The station-keeper moved away from the door to face Carlsen.

98

'Mr Carlsen, I don't know what the hell you're doin', but the stage company's gonna kick your butt for this. These gentlemen are under the protection of the company.'

Carlsen ignored him. He raised his Colt. 'OK, take off your hats.' As he saw the men hesitate he swung the Colt along the line. 'Take 'em off I said, goddamnit!'

Hurriedly, each man raised his hand to pull off his hat. For an instant, Carlsen felt himself freeze, and then he swung around. Two shots sounded, and smoke and the smell of cordite filled the room. Carlsen had an instant to see the red splash of blood across the soldier's face and then the blow to his side hit him like a sledgehammer, sending him staggering. His knees folded and he fell forwards into a black pit, his head crashing against the boards.

'OK, Carlsen, you can put your undershirt back on. You're damned lucky the slug went through. No bones broken, and no vitals hit. You're gonna have another scar you can tell folks about but you'll be fightin' fit in a week or so.'

Dr Wilson, washing his hands in a large bowl placed on the dresser in Carlsen's old room in the Big House of the Bar Circle, looked up as Hector Davis poked his head around the door. A worried frown showed on Davis's face.

'OK to come in now, Doctor?'

'Fine. Give Carlsen a coupla minutes and if Miss Nicholls is back from town, she can come an' see the patient.' He reached over to dry his hands on the towel from the rail at the side of the dresser.

Davis opened the door wider and entered the room to look down on Carlsen, who was seated in the centre of the room, pulling on his shirt.

'Mrs Gittins'll bring you coffee. Laker was alive when the stage brought you both back into town but he died before saying anything.'

'I guess I was lucky a stage was comin' south.'

'And you were lucky I was in town with the doctor.'

'He'd have lasted a while,' Wilson said. 'I reckon it'll take more than a wingin' from a pocket pistol to finish Carlsen.'

'Keep thinkin' like that, Doc,' Carlsen said wryly.

He began to struggle to his feet as the door opened wider and Jane Nicholls stood in the doorway. 'May I come in?'

'All finished here, Miss Nicholls,' Wilson said. He picked up his bag. 'I'll send you my bill.'

'How is Sean?'

Wilson looked thoughtful. 'It'll take time. You'll not get him back this summer but plenty of rest and he'll be fine.'

'I'll see you to your buggy,' Davis said.

Jane Nicholls moved to take the seat opposite Carlsen as the two men left the room. 'I told the sheriff that Laker was the man who met me in the hotel.' She looked puzzled for a moment. 'Was he really a soldier?'

Carlsen shook his head. 'Just a quick-thinkin' feller. He musta used that uniform before. He was tryin' to make sure he got out of town before somebody caught up with him.'

'And you did,' she said, and smiled.

Carlsen's hand moved to touch the bulge beneath his shirt where Wilson had strapped a thick wedge of cotton. 'He almost fooled me with that soldier's uniform.' His mouth twitched. 'But we're no further ahead. The sheriff bringing you that letter troubles me but Fenner is as straight as a wagon tongue. I'll go into town tomorrow an' ask him about it.'

'I thought Dr Wilson said you should rest.'

'No time for that, Miss Jane. Ol' man Hendrix is tryin' to run you off this place an' I'm aimin' to stop him.'

The sun had been up for a couple of hours the next

morning when Carlsen left the trail and joined the hard-pack which led him between the bathhouse and billiards saloon and along Main Street. Several of the townsmen called out to him as he passed and he acknowledged their greetings, guessing they had seen him being carried from the stage and on to the wagon that took him out to the ranch.

He reached the sheriff's office and stepped down from his mount carefully, anxious not to pull at the strapping on his side. He'd been lucky, he knew, but he'd been shot before and knew that if the wound didn't go bad, he'd be fine in a short while. He stepped up to the boardwalk and pushed open the sheriff's door. Fenner was behind his desk, writing in a large journal. He put down his pen as Carlsen stepped into the office.

'Just tellin' the marshal 'bout you,' he said. He gestured to the heavy-set man standing up and thrusting out his hand towards Carlsen.

'Robert Payne,' the marshal introduced himself. 'You coulda seen me hereabouts last year.'

Carlsen shook his head. 'At this time I reckon to be with the beef. But I'm glad you're around. The sheriff tol' you about Hendrix trying to take over the Bar Circle?'

'I've heard a coupla things but there's nothin' to get me involved.'

'My owner, a real gentlewoman, was bushwhacked. Ain't that business fer a marshal?'

'Sure it is, but I hear you've taken care of that an' the lady's back safe and well.'

'It ain't gonna finish there. Old man Hendrix's a land-hungry sonovabitch.'

'Well, Mr Carlsen, that ain't a crime. If I lock up every land-hungry rancher in Wyoming, we'd need to build more jails. But any no-good commits a crime outside the sheriff's

101

jurisdiction, you can be sure I'll be after him.'

'Help yourself to coffee, Jack,' Fenner said. 'You're lookin' a mite paper-backed.'

'I'm OK, but I'll take the coffee.'

He crossed to the stove, took down a mug from a hook on the stucco wall and poured himself coffee. Coming back to the chair alongside the marshal, he took a sip of the hot, black liquid, and immediately felt better. He'd found the ride into town harder going than he'd expected.

'She's a fine lady, your Miss Jane, brave, too,' Fenner said. 'Took one look at that Laker feller, face all broken up, and said straightaways that he took her away from the hotel. Some of the ladies who've been out west for a while woulda swooned.'

'You took a letter out to her a few days ago.'

'Yeah, I was goin' out to see Hendrix and passin' your spread. The letter was fer your Miss Jane.'

Carlsen's mouth twitched. 'The lady ain't my Miss Jane, but no matter. That letter set up Laker to take her away.'

Fenner frowned. 'You ain't thinkin' I got anythin' to do with that?'

Carlsen shook his head. 'No, but it'd help if I knew how you got hold of the letter.'

'That's no problem. I found it on my desk. I figured that some feller knew I was passin' that way an' left it fer me to deliver.'

CHAPTER TEN

Davis's expression showed he was uneasy. He and Carlsen were seated in the parlour in the Big House of the ranch, and the lawyer had been voicing his concern about Carlsen's plans for the day.

'You sure you know what you're doing, Jack? You heard Dr Wilson's advice that you should take it easy for a couple of days.'

'Walter Hendrix is no fool,' Carlsen said. 'Sure, he's land-hungry but he'll not risk a range war. He must know you could bring in the Pinkertons.' Carlsen frowned. 'But cowboys from both ranches are gonna get killed if any shootin' starts. So I'm gonna ride over to the Lazy Y an' see if I can parley with him.'

Davis nodded. 'If you're feeling OK, then that sounds fine. Don't make him any promises we can't keep, Jack. If he starts talking about buying the Bar Circle, tell him you have to report back to JB.'

Carlsen grinned. 'Don't worry, Hector. I sure ain't gonna risk a tongue-lashing.'

An hour later, Carlsen rode away from the Bar Circle. His shoulder ached but it was far from being the worst wound he'd suffered. He wasn't planning to dwell on it but he knew he'd been lucky to have his gun in his hand when he turned to face Laker. He pushed it from his mind and settled to enjoy the morning. Good weather in Wyoming didn't last long and he'd learned to make the best of it.

Save for his seeing a distant rider probably making for Jensen, his ride to the Hendrix spread passed without incident. A few minutes before noon, he rode beneath a weather-beaten board, proclaiming that he was now on Lazy Y land. An hour later, he reached the Big House.

He'd been there several times over the previous five or six years. When the railroad had arrived in Jensen, there'd been some argument over who was going to load their beef first. It had taken two or three days of hard talk before it was sorted out to the satisfaction of both ranches. Carlsen looked around. The layout was similar to that of the Bar Circle. A cluster of barns and corrals surrounded the Big House in front of which stood a hitching rail. He walked his palomino over to the rail, and stepped down from the saddle as the door of house opened. A young woman, her blue dress protected by a white apron, stood looking at him.

'Mr Hendrix has finished his meal but he says you're welcome to join him for coffee.'

'Coffee sounds good,' Carlsen said, as he went up the short steps to the door, unbuckling his gun belt when he stepped into the house behind the young woman. She pointed towards a line of pegs. 'You can leave your belt over there. I'll show you through.'

Walter Hendrix was seated at a table with chairs for a dozen places, although the polished wood of the table was bare, save for a large china cup and saucer in front of the rancher and an open box of cigarillos.

'Millie, get Mr Carlsen coffee,' he ordered. Hendrix waved to a chair on the long side of the table. 'Take a seat, Carlsen. What brings you to the Lazy Y?'

Carlsen didn't reply immediately, waiting until Millie had

returned with a cup and saucer matching those in front of Hendrix. From a metal pot she poured coffee halfway up the cup.

'You can go now, Millie,' Hendrix said. 'I'll call if I need you.'

The door closed behind the young woman and Hendrix stared hard at Carlsen. 'I guess you ain't here to ask after my health. So speak out.'

Carlsen took a few moments before speaking. He knew Hendrix had a fierce temper. There would be little to gain by not choosing his words carefully.

'A no-good by the name o' Laker an' three of his side-kicks took away Miss Jane Nicholls. Someways she was tricked into thinkin' she was gonna talk to the Ladies Society in town. They took her outta the back of the hotel an' travelled to the old nester's spread an' put her in a shanty your men are now using. Me an' my partner had to get her back safe.' His fingers touched his shoulder. 'An' later I got shot by Laker. I figure the whole business was tied in with you tryin' to get your hands on the Bar Circle.'

Hendrix's face darkened. 'What the hell you talkin' about?'

'I'm gonna come clean,' Carlsen said. 'I came here to talk about the chances of our two ranches gettin' to fightin'. I've seen a range war once an' I never wanna see one agin.'

Carlsen expected the rancher to bellow at him again but to his surprise Hendrix pushed the cigarillos across the table. 'Here, take one.'

Carlsen wasn't all that inclined to the harsh tobacco of cigarillos but he needed time to think. Hendrix's reaction had surprised him. He was willing to wager that Hendrix was hearing about Jane's misadventures for the first time. Had he got the rancher all wrong? Was there someone else who was planning to move in on the Bar Circle? Hendrix wanted the Bar Circle for beef and more land to call his own but was there someone who was hoping to make a quick profit from driving away Jane Nicholls? He bent his head, the cigarillo clamped between his teeth to take the light from the match Hendrix was holding towards him.

'Then we're playin' the same hand,' Hendrix said. 'We don't need to get fightin'. We both got good men an' we don't wanna see any killed.'

'You know anythin' about three shootists? One of 'em favours a beard down to his vest.'

Hendrix shook his head. 'Don't mean anythin' to me.'

'But you did buy the guns o' three no-goods from the saloon.'

Hendrix waved his hand dismissively. 'You can forget them. My son hired them. Grant tol' me we'd had trouble with rustlers an' he didn't want our cowboys gettin' in the line o' fire.'

'He didn't hire them to scare off the nesters?'

'Nobody scared off the nesters. They just upped an' left.'

'It didn't happen like that. The Ford family were told they'd be killed if they didn't go.'

Hendrix took the cigar from his mouth and stabbed the air with it in Carlsen's direction. 'Now you just hold on. My son tol' me what happened. The nesters left because that's what they wanted.'

'Then your son was lying to you,' Carlsen said.

There was a second of silence around the table. Then Hendrix exploded, his face puce with rage. He heaved his enormous bulk from his chair, glowering down at Carlsen. 'Goddamnit, Carlsen! You sit at my table and tell me my son is a liar?'

Carlsen got to his feet. 'I gotta young feller who was there when his kinfolk were threatened. You put a hobble on Grant or he's gonna end up gettin' himself into a whole passel o' trouble.'

'Get outta here, Carlsen!' Hendrix yelled, his face blood-red. 'Get out o' my house while you're still standin'!'

'I've tol' you once, Hendrix. I ain't gonna tell you agin.'

Carlsen turned on his heel and strode from the room. A few moments later he was stepping up to his palomino. As he rode away from the house he heard Hendrix bawl, 'Millie! Tell my son I wanna see him!'

As Carlsen trotted his palomino the last hundred yards to the Big House of the Bar Circle, he saw a chestnut hitched to the rail in front of the house. The muscles across his back tightened. The fancy red reins secured to the pommel of the chestnut's saddle told him who was visiting. Grant Hendrix must have been the distant rider he'd seen during his ride that morning. But what was he doing here?

He stepped down from his mount and hitched the palomino to the rail. He went into the house and followed the sounds of voices to the open door of the small parlour. Jane was seated in a soft chair on one side of the room. Opposite, stood Grant Hendrix. Carlsen saw that Hendrix was turned out in his best clothes. A trail jacket that had probably never seen a trail, light brown britches tucked into gleaming boots, cavalry-style. Small silver spurs at his heels. He looked freshly shaven and his hair was neatly combed. What the hell was going on here? Surely Hendrix wasn't come courting?

'Howdy, Miss Jane. I didn't mean to cut in.'

'Don't worry, Mr Carlsen. Hector told me where you were planning to ride out. Was your visit successful?'

'I think so, ma'am.'

Jane stood up. 'Mr Hendrix is leaving now. Please show him out.'

'I haven't finished yet.'

107

'But I have, Mr Hendrix. I've given you my answer.' She nodded briefly in the direction of the two men and with a swirl of her skirt, she left the room.

Hendrix glowered across at Carlsen. 'You're a hired hand, Carlsen. You're gonna stick your nose in once too often.'

'Your mount's at the rail,' Carlsen said evenly.

He turned and led the way to the door, pausing while Hendrix took down his gun belt and buckled it around his waist. Then he opened the door and stepped out.

'I hear you said anythin' not right to Miss Jane, an' I'm gonna kick your butt all the way to Montana,' he said softly.

Hendrix swung around to face him. 'What's wrong, Carlsen? You want the bitch for yourself?'

Carlsen's clenched fist smashed into his face, sending Hendrix reeling back from the open door across the boards, and pitching him on to the hardpack. Hendrix rolled over on to his back, cursing, his hand reaching for his sidearm.

'I'm not carryin', Hendrix,' Carlsen shouted, his arms away from his sides. 'An' you pull that gun on Bar Circle land an' I'll have you hanged on the spot.'

Hendrix scrambled to his feet, his face burning red. 'There was a place for you, Carlsen,' he snarled. 'But no more! Afore you end up beggin' fer work, you an' me are gonna settle accounts an' we'll not be shootin' at some wooden targets!'

He turned his back and strode to his horse. A few moments later, Carlsen watched him kick his horse into a gallop, riding away from the Bar Circle.

Carlsen stood, shaking his hand to ease his knuckles. Punching a man on the jaw was the quickest way to end up with a broken hand. He'd learned that lesson a long time ago. And obviously forgotten it, he told himself wryly.

108

'I saw you knock him down.' Jane spoke from behind Carlsen. 'What was that about?'

'Nothing for you to worry about, Miss Jane. Grant Hendrix gets a mite ornery when he can't get what he wants.'

'And he wanted me.'

Carlsen swung around on his heel. 'What?'

'He asked me to marry him. He said that he would inherit the Lazy Y, and if I were to marry him we'd have one of the biggest spreads in the Territory. I could raise money in the east and we could bring in Hereford bulls from England and more cattle from the south.' A smile played around her lips. 'I'm not sure he spoke of my womanly virtues.'

Carlsen snorted. 'I threatened to kick him into Montana. That wasn't far enough.'

Jane's smile grew broader. 'Hector is in the parlour. Come and tell us what happened at the Lazy Y.'

Both Hector and Jane listened attentively to Carlsen as he described his meeting with Walter Hendrix. When he'd finished, Hector was obviously puzzled. 'You really think he was hearing about JB's misadventures for the first time?'

'I guess that's so.'

'Could it be Grant Hendrix behind all this trouble?'

'But that doesn't make sense, Hector,' Jane said. 'Why would he have me taken away and then soon after ask to marry me?'

Hector Davis's eyes bulged. 'He did what?'

'I haven't had time to mention it to you. Yes, Mr Hendrix suggested that if I were to marry him we would be the biggest ranchers in this part of the Territory.'

Davis almost snorted. 'I am a distinguished New York lawyer,' he said loudly, addressing the ceiling. 'Since arriving in Wyoming, I've been involved in a barroom brawl. I

109

spend each morning pitching hay, my most valuable client and dear friend has been rescued from evil men and is now being wooed by an ignorant cowboy.'

Jane laughed. 'Welcome to life in the West, Hector!'

Carlsen stood up. 'If you'll excuse me, Miss Jane, I need to take a look in the barn. Tomorrow I'm plannin' to take a ride up to the beef, see everythin's goin' fine, an' Pete Maxton's got everything fixed.'

'I'll ride along with you,' Jane said.

'I don't think that's a good notion, ma'am.'

'I'm sure you'll keep me safe from any assassin,' she said briskly.

'Jack didn't mean that,' Davis said. 'The cattle have moved for the summer. You'll not reach them and return in one day.'

'I'll be sleepin' 'neath the stars, Miss Jane,' Carlsen added.

'Then I shall sleep beneath the stars, too,' Jane said promptly.

'For pity's sake, JB!' Davis sounded shocked. 'Think of your reputation! People back east hear of such a notion and you'll not be received in polite society.'

'Oh, fiddlesticks, Hector. You're too concerned with my reputation. We'll ride out after breakfast, Mr Carlsen. Have Ethan saddle the chestnut. I shall not require the side-saddle.' Without waiting for an answer, she turned on her heel and left the two men standing speechless.

CHAPTER ELEVEN

The following morning, Carlsen and Mather were eating breakfast in Carlsen's shanty. Carlsen put down his fork on the rough-hewn table and looked hard at his old partner. 'You sure about what you're doin', Hank? There's a place for you here at the Bar Circle if you want it.'

Mather chewed on his beans for a few seconds. Then he shook his head. 'What would I do at a ranch, Jack? I'm too old to learn about beef an' the work of a ranch. I know my long gun, my Colt, an' a scatter-gun. An' that's it. There's no place for me here.'

'Fer chris'sakes, Hank. This ain't '65. You're right, we ain't gettin' any younger. Wyoming's soon gonna be a State. There'll be no place for a feller in a saloon or a cat-house with a scatter-gun 'cross his knees, keeping the peace. Stay in Jensen. Run a store or somethin' like you said.'

Mather let out a bellow of laughter. 'Sure, I can jest see me cuttin' curtains fer the Reverend's wife. No, Jack, I know you mean well but I'm gonna take off fer Cheyenne an' that pile o' dollars Mr Davis gave me.'

'You earned 'em, Hank.' Carlsen stood up, and held out his hand. 'Mebbe I'll see you in Cheyenne, come the winter.'

Mather, too, stood up. He shook Carlsen's hand. 'Don't

111

fergit you said that.'

'C'mon, I gotta see Ethan. You can get your horse.'

When the two men walked into the barn they were greeted by a cheerful Ethan. 'Got your mount saddled an' ready to go, Mr Mather. Miss Jane's chestnut is fine, an' your palomino's rarin' to go, Mr Carlsen.'

'OK, Ethan.'

Carlsen raised a hand as Mather mounted his horse. 'Keep your head down, Hank.'

'Sure will.' Mather gave him a mock salute, turned his horse's head, and rode away from the Bar Circle.

Carlsen watched him for a moment and then turned on his heel and entered the barn. He needed to check that Ethan had fed and watered the dozen horses they kept in their own stalls. He needn't have concerned himself. The horses were all chewing contentedly at their hay-bags. From behind the barn came the sound of an axe cutting into wood, and Carlsen guessed Ethan was about his morning's tasks. He walked along the barn to pull gently at his palomino's ears and allow the horse to lick at his hand.

Hector Davis was at the far end of the barn, hoisting bales of hay on to boards. Carlsen couldn't help being amused at this important lawyer with offices back east, who was wiping the sweat off his forehead with a large, coloured neckerchief, a hayfork in one hand. He had to give Hector his due. The lawyer had stuck to his task and was now filling out with the exercise, his face showing the colour of his days in the sun.

'How's the work goin', Hector?' Carlsen called.

Davis pushed his neckerchief into a pocket of his bib coveralls. 'Fine, Jack. Gets easier every day. How's your shoulder?'

'Aches like a bitch but it'll get better. Have Ethan get the horses ready to go in an hour. I'll see Mrs Gittins an' fix some grub.'

An hour later, Carlsen and Jane rode away from the Big House. Ethan, without being told, had rolled up a blanket and a rain-slicker and lashed them both to Jane's saddle. In Carlsen's saddle bag, wrapped in a clean cloth, were two pieces of beef, bacon, beans and half a dozen biscuits. Both riders had filled their canteens from the barrel of water in the kitchen of the Big House.

'I reckon on five hours ridin',' Carlsen said, as the horses trotted along. 'We'll take a break at noon, an' be with the beef by mid-afternoon.'

He looked across at Jane. 'You sure look purty in that Stetson, ma'am.'

Jane smiled, touching the hat with a gloved hand. 'I found it a couple of days ago. I think it must have belonged to my grandmother. The sun's getting stronger. I've no wish to go back east with a face like a homesteader.'

'Your gran'ma an' Mr Jackson would be mighty proud that the Bar Circle's gonna prosper in your hands, Miss Jane.'

'Only if my plans work out, Mr Carlsen.'

Before Carlsen could ask what she was planning, Jane had urged her chestnut forward, and he guessed that now was not the time to be asking questions. He knew she wouldn't consider Grant Hendrix's offer of marriage for a second but he reckoned anything else was possible.

They took a break at noon, not setting a fire for coffee but instead taking water from their canteens. Jane pulled out a small, leather-backed book and began writing. Carlsen threw himself full stretch on the buffalo grass, tipped his hat over his eyes and slept for half an hour. When he awoke, he was conscious of Jane looking at him intently from a few feet away.

'You OK, Miss Jane?'

'I am very well, Mr Carlsen.' Her steady gaze remained. 'Did you know I spoke with Mr Mather for a while last night?'

Carlsen shook his head.

'Mr Mather told me about you both in the War, and how you led him and those twenty men at Petersburg, keeping them all alive when your officer was killed.'

'Hank always did talk too much. Anyways, it was a long time ago.'

She continued as if he hadn't spoken. 'And how you both worked for Pinkerton's after the War until those people were killed at Green Valley.'

Carlsen climbed to his feet. 'An' it was my fault they were killed, Miss Jane. Did Mather tell you that?' His face set, he walked towards his horse without looking back.

They saw the chuck-wagon outlined against the steel blue sky a couple of hours after noon. As if anticipating a feed and a rest from the loping pace of the previous two hours, the horses quickened their pace. Soon the half-a-dozen men around the wagon held up their hands in greeting, calling a welcome.

'Howdy, Miss Jane. Howdy, Mr Carlsen.'

Carlsen stepped down from his palomino, holding a hand out for Jane to step down to the buffalo grass. 'Howdy, boys. All fine with the beef?'

'Pete Maxton's a coupla miles on,' said one. 'Reckon the beef's settled for the summer.'

'And the men?' Jane asked. 'Is all well?'

Three or four of the cowboys exchanged glances. 'Good of you to ask, Miss Jane. Yeah, we're all fine.'

'I'm pleased to hear that.' Jane raised her head a couple of inches. 'Is that coffee I smell?'

A bulky, broad-shouldered man with a grey canvas apron covering his range clothes stepped forwards. 'They call me

Cookie, ma'am. I've just made coffee for the boys,' he said.

Carlsen grinned. 'You drink that coffee, Miss Jane, an' it's gonna take your breath away,' he said.

'If it's good enough for the men, it's good enough for me,' she said, with a smile which grew as the men around her let out a cheer. Cookie, having found a mug which he'd wiped on a cloth, brought across the coffee.

Jane took a sip and Carlsen grinned broadly as he saw her expression.

'My, that's strong, Cookie, but it's delicious.'

Well, that's Cookie signed on to the list of men who'd go out and die for their new owner, Carlsen thought. While Jane drank her coffee and chatted in a friendly fashion to three or four of the cowboys, Carlsen retrieved both his and Jane's canteens and filled them from the barrel at the rear of the wagon. He returned the canteens to their saddle-bags and turned to Jane.

'Best be gettin' along, ma'am,' he said.

She handed her mug to Cookie. 'Thank you, I enjoyed that.'

Cookie tugged at the brim of his battered hat. 'A pleasure to serve you, ma'am.'

As Carlsen and Jane rode away from the wagon, Carlsen turned his head towards the young woman. 'You handle the men well, Miss Jane.'

'I know how those men work hard for me,' she said. 'They deserve courtesy.'

If only her uncle had had the same notions, maybe the Bar Circle wouldn't be struggling, Carlsen reckoned. If Jane Nicholls invested more money there was a good chance the ranch would survive. He knew there'd been talk among the men last winter about quitting and finding a job at a more prosperous ranch. He reckoned all that was beginning to change. Cowboys were quick to recognize an owner who gave them his or her support. Miss Jane Nicholls, he reck-oned, could count on a loyal bunch.

After a ride of maybe half an hour, they passed the out-lying animals, both Carlsen and Jane waving to the men riding at the edge of the herd who were making sure the animals were settled and making the most of the rich grass.

'There's Pete Maxton,' Carlsen said, pointing out a lone rider wearing a yellow slicker. He grinned. 'Pete always reckons it's gonna rain in the next few minutes. He's a good man an' we're lucky he's stuck with the Bar Circle.'

They trotted their mounts between the grazing cattle until they reached Maxton, who stood in his stirrups to greet them.

'Pete, this lady is Miss Jane, the new owner.'

Maxton's eyes flicked to Jane Nicholls's riding pants, his expression carefully neutral. Then he tugged at the brim of his Stetson. 'A pleasure to meet you, ma'am. The boys speak well of you an' they're hopin' for better times ahead.'

'I intend to make that happen, Mr Maxton.' She shifted in her saddle as if to dismount, but Carlsen cut in.

'Stay on your horse, Miss Jane. Some of these cattle can be ornery but they'll not trouble you if you're in the saddle.'

She gave a brief nod and eased back.

'You thinkin' of bringin' in Herefords, ma'am?' Maxton asked.

Jane smiled. 'More for me to learn, Mr Maxton. I don't even know what Herefords are.'

'They're English cattle, Miss Jane,' Carlsen explained. 'Folks across at Powder River crossed them with longhorns. Reckon they're gettin' hardy animals along with the good beef of the Herefords.'

'Problem is,' Maxton added, 'Hereford bulls cost a whole heap o' dollars.'

Jane nodded but made no comment.

'Any more beef disappeared?' Carlsen asked.

Maxton shook his head. 'Two or three o' the ex-army boys we got have been lookin' 'round. I reckon any no-goods have moved on.'

Or gone back to the Lazy Y, Carlsen thought. But he merely nodded.

'Good to hear. I'm leavin' you in charge, Pete. Miss Jane wants me down at the house an' I know you can handle everythin' up here.'

Maxton merely nodded but it was obvious he was pleased.

'Me an' Miss Jane oughtta be gettin' back.'

'Thank you for all your good work, Mr Maxton.'

Maxton tugged at the brim of his hat. 'A pleasure, ma'am. I reckon the Bar Circle's gonna be fine now.'

Jane and Carlsen trotted their mounts in the direction of the chuck wagon, Carlsen explaining that the railroad spur from the town to Cheyenne now made it much easier to bring in bulls from anywhere in the country and from Europe.

'We pay the money, Miss Jane,' Carlsen said, 'an' some feller will bring us the bulls.'

'Then we shall—' She broke off, pointing ahead to the chuck wagon with her short whip. 'Is that Sheriff Fenner speaking with Cookie?'

'An' that's Marshal Payne with him. What they doin' here?'

'Howdy, Miss Jane.' Fenner greeted her as Jane and Carlsen joined the group of men around the wagon. He stared hard at Carlsen. 'We got a coupla questions for you, Jack.'

'Marshal Payne, ma'am.' The lawman introduced himself. 'You don't haveta listen to what we're gonna talk about.'

'Mr Carlsen works for me, Marshal. If you have questions for him I wish to hear them.'

'But, ma'am—'

Jane rapped her short whip against her boot. 'Ask your questions, Marshal. Mr Carlsen and I wish to be on our way.'

Payne nodded briefly, clearly annoyed, but seemingly reluctant to clash with the owner of a large ranch.

'Very well, ma'am.' He turned to Carlsen. 'I'm told you rode over to the Lazy Y yesterday. You gonna tell me why you did that?'

'Sure. I tol' you the other day ol' man Hendrix reckons he can take over the Bar Circle. Laker, the feller who took away Miss Jane, was jest a hired hand. If he'd have lived, I reckon he might have said it was Hendrix who'd hired him.'

'So you rode over to the Lazy Y to settle accounts?'

'I saw Hendrix to tell him he was riskin' a range war and none of us wanted that. Men can get killed, cowboys who'd never pull a gun end up gettin' lynched. I've seen it happen an' I don't wanna see it agin.'

'I guess that musta made Hendrix mad,' Fenner said. 'Him an' you bawlin' at each other.'

'Yeah, somethin' like that.' Carlsen frowned. 'Where's this leadin', Marshal?'

'Hendrix was found dead behind his desk by his son. I've seen the body myself,' Payne said. 'A slug through his brain.' He tapped the right side of his head.

'So he didn't kill himself,' Jane said.

Payne frowned, apparently put out by an interruption from a young woman, ranch owner or not. 'What makes you say that, ma'am?'

'Walter Hendrix was left-handed. I noticed when he took coffee with me.'

Carlsen resisted the temptation to smile at the reddening of the marshal's face. 'Anyways,' he said, 'what's the shootin' got to do with us?'

Payne looked across at Fenner and nodded.

The sheriff reached into his pocket and took out a pocket pistol. 'The shootist dropped his weapon when he took to his heels.' He stared hard at Carlsen and then turned over the butt of the .22. The small blue stone gleamed in the afternoon sun. 'Looks like one I've seen you carry, Jack.'

A deep frown marked Jane's face. 'Now just a—'

'It's OK, Miss Jane.'

Carlsen dug his hand into the deep pocket of his trail jacket and pulled out the .22 pistol he'd bought a few days earlier from the General Store. He held it so both Fenner and Payne could see the butt. He turned it over slowly. The sun glinted on the blue glass.

'Any o' those no-goods from the Silver Dollar near the house yesterday?' he asked, slipping the pistol back into the pocket of his trail jacket.

Fenner frowned, obviously puzzled. 'Why would they be out at the Lazy Y?'

'Grant Hendrix hired 'em a while back. Used 'em to drive off the nesters.'

'Maybe you should be asking more questions at the Lazy Y, Marshal,' said Jane sharply. 'I assume Mr Carlsen and I can now return home.'

Payne touched the brim of his Stetson. 'Of course, ma'am. I'm sorry we troubled you.'

Jane gave a brief nod. 'We shall be late for our supper, Mr Carlsen, if we don't press on.'

She swung around in her saddle to wave farewell to the bunch of cowboys who had stood some hundred yards away, plainly curious about what was going on. Their raised hands and shouts wishing her good fortune were a pleasant interruption to Carlsen's thoughts of his lost pocket pistol. Had the weapon ended up in the possession of one of the no-goods from the saloon, or was there another explanation? There was no riding around it. That fancy pocket pistol was going to cause him a heap of trouble. With Jane Nicholls present, Payne was stepping softly. When he or Fenner chased down the pistol, it would be a different story.

Carlsen and Jane trotted their horses along, Carlsen heading in the direction of a stand of cottonwoods that he knew ringed a stretch of water that was clear and safe to drink. Neither rider said anything, both lost in their own thoughts of the news that had been brought to them by the two lawmen.

Finally, Carlsen knew he had to speak. He edged his mount closer to Jane's chestnut. 'I gotta problem, Miss Jane.'

'The pistol that the sheriff showed us,' she said. 'Was it yours?'

'Now how in tarnation did you know that?'

'I think it was because you didn't lie. You said nothing and allowed them to decide.'

Carlsen's mouth twitched. 'I hope you never take up poker, ma'am.' His half smile disappeared. 'I'm gonna haveta tell Fenner. That pistol I showed him and the marshal was one of a matching pair. I reckon the one they have was the one I lost last year. The marshal was plannin' to throw me in jail, an' I couldn't take that chance with you and Hector to protect.'

'You think we need protecting?'

'With his father dead, Grant Hendrix will be callin' the shots. I know he drove off the nesters an' I reckon he led the passel o' gunslingers when Grant Hendrix took over the old Double B. He's gonna start thinkin' he could do the same with the Bar Circle.'

'Mr Carlsen, did you kill Walter Hendrix?'

'No, ma'am, I did not. An' I unn'erstand why you had to ask me. There's no hard feelin's about it.' He looked ahead and pointed with an outstretched arm. 'There's the cottonwoods I've been headin' for. We'll have a fire goin' in no time.'

A couple of hours later, they sat alongside each other, eating the beef and beans Carlsen had fried in the pan he'd taken from his saddlebag. He rested his fork on the side of the tin plate while he picked up a small piece of wood and threw it on the fire which burned strongly, throwing out heat against the cool air of the Wyoming night. Behind Carlsen, his bedroll had been placed on the ground. On the opposite side of the fire, Jane had unrolled her own, ready for when they finished eating.

'My mama would swoon away if she could see me now,' Jane said, with a laugh. 'But it's great fun.'

'Heck, Miss Jane, all we're doin' is havin' supper.'

'I shall tell all my girlfriends how I sat out alone at night in cattle country eating supper around a fire with a real cowboy.'

Carlsen grinned. 'Then they'll think you're no longer a lady.'

Again, Jane laughed. 'No, no. They will be green with envy.' She suddenly looked serious. 'I have to go back to New York next month, Mr Carlsen. When Hector and I arrived in Jensen Flats, we expected to be leaving after a week or so. Hector was planning to put the ranch in the hands of the town's lawyer.' She smiled. 'I guess I must follow my grandfather, after all.'

The beef in Carlsen's stomach seemed suddenly to weigh heavier. 'So what are you plannin', Miss Jane?'

'I shall try to take over the Lazy Y. Hector reckons that both ranches are too small to make any serious money.

Hector will raise the money in New York when we return.'

'Grant Hendrix will never sell.'

'He will if the price is right.' She took a forkful of the beans alongside the piece of beef. 'Is the Hendrix range boss a good man?'

'Sam Marley is one of the best,' Carlsen said promptly.

She turned her head to look at him. 'Could Maxton take over your job as range boss of the Bar Circle?'

He was silent for a few moments. Then he spoke more loudly than he'd intended. 'Yeah, he could. An' what do I do? Go east with you an' Hector an' look after your horses so you'll have a real cowboy 'bout the place?'

Jane threw back her head and laughed. 'Honestly, Mr Carlsen, you are sometimes priceless!' She put down her plate on the ground beside her. 'No, Mr Carlsen,' and her eyes sparkled in the light from the fire, 'when I return east, I want you to move back into the Big House. What's the expression I've heard you use? I want you to be the top *honcho* of the two ranches.'

For a few seconds, he was unable to speak. Above him the sky was like a black velvet cloth sprinkled with precious stones. When he'd first been hired by Jackson Nicholls, he'd been glad of a job that meant he could put his old life behind him. The first years hadn't been easy for him. Folks out east thought the life of a cowboy was free and easy, but he'd soon learned that work on a cattle ranch could be hard going. But he'd stuck at it. And if Grant Hendrix did sell out now that his father was dead, Miss Jane was offering him his reward.

'You're willin' to trust me that much?'

'I trust you, Hector trusts you, and the men trust you. I know you can find your place when you meet other cattle-men down in Cheyenne.'

'Some of 'em are just moneymen. I know as much about

beef as the others.'

'Of course, you'll need a respectable wife.'

He hitched himself up on one elbow. In the light of the flames he could detect the mischievous glint in her eyes as she looked back at him across the fire.

'I sure hope matchmakin' ain't part o' your plans, Miss Jane.'

CHAPTER TWELVE

After breakfast of bacon and beans, Carlsen and Jane headed for the Bar Circle. Neither spoke, both seemingly lost in their own thoughts as the two horses loped along, closing the distance to the ranch at a steady pace.

The marshal and Fenner had ridden out from Jensen, meaning to take him to jail. Of that Carlsen was sure. The sheriff had recognized the pocket pistol found at the Lazy Y and recalled where he'd seen it before. Marshal and Fenner would question Tom Rudman in the General Store and they'd learn that Rudman had sold him the second of a matching pair. Would Fenner believe that he'd lost the pistol the previous year? His thoughts were interrupted by Jane bringing her mount closer and slowing the animal to a trot. He reined in to have his palomino match the pace.

'You're very quiet this morning, Mr Carlsen.'

'I reckon I need to ride into Jensen once we get back to the ranch. That marshal could railroad me into a lynchin' party if I ain't smart. I'll tell Fenner I wasn't tryin' to fool him but I had to get you home safe.'

'Should you have Hector with you?'

'That'll make them think I've got somethin' to hide.' His

mouth twisted. 'I'll only need Hector if they throw me in a cage.'

They reached the Bar Circle a couple of hours before noon. As they walked their horses across the hardpack in front of the Big House, Ethan ran out from the barn to greet them. Carlsen stepped down from the saddle.

'A good clean an' then a feed,' he ordered.

'Sure thing, boss. How was sleepin' 'neath the stars, Miss Jane?'

Jane took Carlsen's hand as she dismounted. 'Not as romantic as dime novels pretend,' she said, smiling. She rubbed at the small of her back and rolled her shoulders. 'I prefer a soft mattress and cotton sheets.' She looked at Carlsen. 'Do you still mean to ride into town?'

'Yes, Miss Jane. It's fer the best.'

'Very well. I'll see you when you return.'

Ethan and Carlsen watched her climb the steps and enter the Big House.

'She's some lady,' Ethan said admiringly.

'You're damn right, Ethan. Now get me another horse an' saddle her up while I see Mrs Gittins fer coffee.'

Carlsen was three or four miles from the Bar Circle when he saw the buggy heading along the trail towards him. At the distance, he couldn't tell if the driver was a man or a woman. He felt the muscles tighten across his back. Not many folks drove a buggy out to the Bar Circle. Was it the doctor with bad news about Sean? But as the buggy drew closer, he was relieved to see that the driver was a woman. Maybe a caller for Miss Jane.

They'd be in for a wait. He guessed that his new owner was on that soft mattress and beneath those cotton sheets she'd talked about. As the buggy drew closer he recognized the driver as Eliza Parsons. A smile touched his lips, remembering the words of Miss Jane the previous night.

'Howdy, Eliza,' he greeted her, touching the brim of his Stetson as both his mount and the buggy drew to a halt alongside each other. 'Miss Jane is at the ranch if you're hopin' to see her. But she's restin'. We've been out with the beef fer a day or so.' He looked at her face, unusually grim. 'Anythin' wrong, Eliza?'

'It's not Miss Jane I'm calling on,' she said. 'It's you I've come to see, Jack.'

'Well now, that's always a pleasure,' he said lightly.

'You mustn't go into town, Jack,' she cut in. 'Marshal Payne has given orders that the sheriff is to put you in jail if you come in.'

Carlsen frowned. 'That don't make sense. If the marshal wants me in jail, he coulda come out to the Bar Circle hisself.'

'The marshal left town this morning for a couple of days. He had a telegraph message, telling him to return to Cheyenne.'

Carlsen's frown deepened. 'How do you know all this, Eliza?'

'Jim Hartley, the blacksmith, is doing some work for me. He's a Volunteer and told me all the Volunteers have been ordered by the sheriff to keep a look-out for you.'

'You know what this is about?'

'Not really. I only heard that the marshal called on Mr Rudman to ask about a pistol.'

'The pistol found near Walter Hendrix's body,' he said. 'That pistol was mine, Eliza.'

She looked at him for a long moment. 'Then you lost it or somebody stole it from you,' she said. Before Carlsen could reply, she had turned her pony's head and sent the buggy bowling back towards the town.

Carlsen, still turning over in his mind the news from Eliza, walked his palomino across the hardpack in front of the Big House, having taken Eliza's advice and returned to the Bar Circle. He'd talk with Hector Davis before making a move. There was no sense in getting himself locked in the Jensen jail when he needed to be free to find out what was going on.

By the barn, Ethan was talking with a broad-shouldered man who wore leather chaps and Californian spurs. Carlsen had the vague notion that he'd seen him before across at the Lazy Y. Was he here with a message from Grant Hendrix? He stood down to the ground as his horse reached Ethan and the stranger.

'Howdy, Mr Carlsen,' said Ethan cheerfully. 'I'll take your mount. This here feller's come to see you.'

'Chet Morgan from the Lazy Y, Mr Carlsen,' the tall cowboy said. 'I gotta talk with you.'

Carlsen nodded. 'OK, Mr Morgan, we're talkin'. What's all this about?'

Morgan looked over Carlsen's shoulder as if he was anxious that someone was approaching them. He breathed in deeply, and still he said nothing.

'I'm waitin',' Carlsen said.

'I know who killed Walter Hendrix.' Morgan almost spat the words out, his face taut with worry.

Carlsen held up his hand. 'Hold it there.' He turned to Ethan. 'Hitch up my mount, then get on over to Mr Davis. Tell him I'm in the shanty with Mr Morgan.'

'Will do, boss.'

'C'mon, Mr Morgan. Walk over with me an' we'll hear what you gotta say.'

Carlsen and Morgan had taken their seats beside the

table when Hector Davis pushed open the door to the shanty. Close behind, Ethan carried three mugs of coffee. He placed them on the table and left the shanty as Davis took the remaining seat.

'What's all this about, Jack?'

'Mr Morgan's from the Lazy Y. He's got some news for us.' He nodded to the Lazy Y hand. 'Go ahead. Mr Davis is a lawyer so you just say what you know.'

Morgan took a mouthful of coffee looking first at Carlsen and then at Davis, before clearing his throat. 'I was doin' some work on the barn near the Big House. I was high up an' could see into Mr Hendrix's room where he had his desk. I saw Mr Carlsen arrive an' I saw him leave after talkin' with Mr Hendrix.'

'Did you see Hendrix alive after I left?' Carlsen asked.

'Sure, I did. He was in front of the big door when Grant Hendrix arrived.'

'What happened next?' Davis asked.

'They went into the house. I couldn't see 'em then but there was a lotta yellin' an' shoutin'. I saw Walter Hendrix in his room an' then Grant Hendrix followin' him. There was more shoutin' an' then Grant Hendrix pulled a gun an' shot his pa.'

'Are you willing to stand up in court and tell a judge what you've told us?' Davis asked.

Morgan's mouth set and he shook his head. 'I aim to live a mite longer. Grant Hendrix hears me talk an' I'll be a dead man. I'm gonna ride south an' leave Wyomin' behind me.'

Davis frowned. 'So why stop here?'

'Grant Hendrix an' his no-goods chased off Ethan's family. Daley Ford was a good friend o' mine.'

Davis leaned back in his chair. 'Grant Hendrix will be looking for you if he thinks you saw the shooting. You'd be safer here overnight and then you can ride on tomorrow.'

Carlsen stood up. 'The men are up with the beef. You'll find a place in the bunkhouse. I'll have Ethan bring you over some chow.'

'Thanks, Mr Carlsen,' Morgan said. 'I'm obliged to you, gentlemen.'

Davis and Carlsen walked back to the Big House, after showing Morgan where he could spend the night.

'You reckon we were right not to hog-tie Morgan?' Carlsen asked the lawyer.

'Give him the night to think about it. He's scared but he wants to do right,' Davis said. 'That's all I need. I'll get him before a judge if I have to carry him.'

The rooster at the back of the barn was greeting the new day when Carlsen opened his eyes. He pushed back the blanket and kicked his legs out to sit at the edge of his bunk. As he pulled on his pants, his first thoughts were of Morgan. Before turning in, he'd instructed Ethan not to have Morgan's horse ready for him to ride out at first light. Over breakfast, he could start the business of persuading the Lazy Y rider to face a judge and say his piece. If Morgan disappeared, he'd have only Hector's word to back him against the marshal producing the pocket pistol.

Ten minutes later, he was walking across to the barn. There was no sign of Morgan's horse and the door to the bunkhouse was still closed. Maybe Morgan was having second thoughts about his chances of avoiding Grant Hendrix or any of the gunslingers Hendrix had taken on his payroll.

He stepped into the barn and saw Ethan appearing from behind one of the stalls halfway along the barn. As he came closer, Carlsen could see that his face was taut, his mouth set. What was going on here?

'I'm sorry, Mr Carlsen. There's nothing—'

Carlsen felt the barrel of a sidearm grind into the back of his neck. The unmistakeable voice of Grant Hendrix was close to his ear. 'Now you just drop that gun belt, Carlsen, an' you might just live another day.'

CHAPTER THIRTEEN

Hendrix snickered. 'An' if you don't, I'll shoot you as a wanted killer tryin' to escape.' He paused, as if turning over the situation in his mind. 'Then I reckon we'd have to kill the kid, so he cain't talk.'

For a second, Carlsen wondered if Hendrix had lost his mind. But no matter; he knew Hendrix, if thwarted, would carry out his threat. His hands dropped to his gun belt, freeing the buckle, allowing the weight of his Colt to drag the belt to the dirt of the barn. He turned around slowly. Behind Hendrix stood the three men who he'd last seen at the old nester's shanty. He stared grimly at the tallest of the three.

'I gave you a chance, Colorado. I tol' you I'd kill you if I saw you 'round these parts agin.'

Before Colorado had a chance to reply Hendrix barked, 'You ain't gonna be killin' anyone, Carlsen. You're gonna be in Fenner's cage and then danglin' at the end of a rope.' He turned to one of the three men. 'Go get our horses. We'll get outta here afore they start movin' in the Big House.'

'You're crazy, Hendrix!' Carlsen exploded. 'There's not a judge in the Territory who'd hang a big rancher for—'

Hendrix's heavy sidearm smashed against the side of

Carlsen's head. His legs gave way, and he crashed on to the dirt. Above him loomed Hendrix. There was a metallic click as the sidearm was cocked.

'Boss! You kill him here an' the law's gonna be after us all.' It was the smallest of the three, his scarred face contorted, who spoke out. For a moment, Hendrix remained still, and then he eased the hammer of his sidearm and lowered his arm.

'I tol' you to bring our horses,' Hendrix ordered. He swung around to face Ethan, who hadn't moved from the centre of the barn. 'Get Carlsen's horse an' no tricks!'

Ten minutes later, Hendrix rode past the Big House, Carlsen behind him, his head down, still feeling the effects of the blow to his head. The three other men rode alongside. Hendrix had chosen his time well. Save for a clattering of pans at the rear of the house where Mrs Gittins and Lucy were starting their day, the ranch house was silent, its occupants still in their beds. Behind them, in the barn, Ethan had been left tied to an old wagon wheel, his neckerchief tight around his mouth as a gag.

'I'm thinkin' we could take the fancy lady with us,' said Colorado. 'There ain't nobody to stop us.'

'You ain't got enough brains to think,' Hendrix snarled. 'You just do what I tell you.'

With a sharp tug on the lead rein from Carlsen's palomino, Hendrix dug his heels into the sides of his mount and took the trail to Jensen Flats.

The side of Carlsen's head throbbed with pain but his mind was clearing as the four men escorted him to Jensen. By the end of the day, he reckoned he'd be in Fenner's jail, awaiting the return of the marshal from Cheyenne and a circuit judge. Hector Davis would need to work hard to save him from swinging at the end of a rope. Townsfolk weren't overly fond of cattlemen but they respected the influence of powerful ranchers and few, if any, would wish to oppose Hendrix in public.

His own purchase of the matching pocket pistol was happenstance but a clever lawyer could make it appear an attempt by a guilty man to cover his tracks. He had to admit Hendrix was playing it smart. By keeping him alive and delivering him to the law he could appear righteous, and make any attempt to take over the Bar Circle that much easier.

'Hey, boss, I thought we was goin' into town?'

The rasping voice of Colorado cut through his thoughts as they reached the fork in the trail, the route to the south leading away from the town. Hendrix swung in his saddle to face Colorado.

'I tol' you once, you think too much. I got somethin' to do afore we take this murderin' no-good into the sheriff. We'll take him in tomorrow when plenty of folks are around. An' remember! Don't rough him up. I want him in one piece when he faces Fenner and the judge.'

Carlsen kept a poker face. He remained silent as Hendrix turned his horse's head and rode away. Did Grant Hendrix know Morgan had seen him shoot his father? Was Hendrix now intending to remove the chance of Morgan appearing before the law by hunting him down and killing him?

Unable to see through the neckerchief covering his eyes, Carlsen felt one of the men untie the saddle string which secured his hands to the pommel of his saddle. Then he was dragged to the ground, his wrists held to prevent him from tearing off the blindfold.

He was pulled away from his horse, heard a door being pushed open and then a shove at his back sent him staggering forwards to fall headlong, his head smashing against a dirt floor. Behind him, the door was banged shut and by the noise, he guessed that a timber had been dropped to make sure it stayed that way.

He tore the neckerchief from his eyes and looked around. There was little light but he could make out that he was in a shanty used as a store, presumably somewhere on Lazy Y land. He felt, more than saw, the rough sacks by his hand and dragged them towards him. If he was kept here overnight, they would provide some protection against the chill of the dirt floor while he slept.

He climbed to his feet. Thankfully the pain in the side of his head had eased. He was thinking straight again and able to weigh up the chances of escape. His own horse had to be tied up somewhere outside the shanty. If he could reach the animal he'd have a chance. Colorado had shoved his gun belt and Colt into the saddlebag of the palomino before they'd quit the Bar Circle.

There could be tools hidden in the dark corners of the shanty but any attempt to break out would alert the three men. Even if they obeyed Hendrix's order not to rough him up, the three would easily overpower him. He'd only be wasting his strength and he'd need to be strong to face the next few days. He lowered himself to the sacks again, shifting around until he found a firm surface against which to lean.

Hector Davis would have found Ethan by now, he realized. Maybe Davis was riding into Jensen to report to Sheriff Fenner. But what could Davis achieve? When Morgan learned that Hendrix had raided the Bar Circle, he'd probably high-tailed it out of the Territory before Hendrix could catch up with him. Without Morgan testifying before a judge, Hendrix would be in the clear.

'An' Jack Carlsen would be at the end of a rope,' Carlsen said aloud.

134

How was Miss Jane taking all of this? For all her beauty and her charm she was a strong young woman. Even if he finished at the end of a rope or breaking rocks down in Cheyenne, the Bar Circle would survive. Of that he was certain. Pete Maxton would take over as range boss. Maybe even move into the Big House when Miss Jane and Hector Davis went back east.

Carlsen breathed in deeply. Thinking of Miss Jane, he could almost smell the fresh flowers of the scent she wore. Despite his situation he managed a brief smile.

'Sure is a fine lady,' he said, again aloud.

Then he breathed in again. The scent of fresh flowers! His hand scrabbled among the sacks on either side of him. His right hand touched soft material. He tugged and it came loose.

He held it to his nose, and knew in that moment where he was being held. The scrap of material in his hand was a scented handkerchief of Miss Jane's. He was in the old Ford shanty where she'd been held. Although he could just about make out the shapes around him, he realized why he hadn't recognized it before. When he and Mather had freed her, she'd appeared at the doorway of the shanty. He hadn't stepped inside.

His mind churned. OK, he knew where he was being held but that didn't help him escape. Or did it? There was something about this shanty that lodged deep in his mind. He sat there for several minutes, clutching the handkerchief against his chin as if the faint scent would sharpen his thoughts.

The day Ethan tried to avenge his pa! What was it he said about this place? 'There's a coupla loose timbers at the back of the shanty.' A grim smile showed on Carlsen's face. He hoped to hell that Ethan's pa hadn't got round to fixing them. He shoved the handkerchief into his pocket and

135

pushed himself to his feet.

He stepped carefully around the crates and tools, and began to feel along the walls of the shanty. Time ticked by. All the timbers appeared to be secure. He was just beginning to think that the Lazy Y hands had worked with hammer and nails after the Fords had left when one of the timbers shifted beneath his hands.

He stood still for a moment as a loud shout of laughter came from outside and he caught the sound of glass against a stone. He judged the men to be about twenty yards from the shanty, maybe setting camp in the lee of the cottonwoods.

Leaning down, he tested a second timber. It shifted. Taking care to avoid the rasp of timber against timber, he made himself enough space to wriggle through the gap on to the buffalo grass at the back of the shanty. Four horses were tied to a rail no more than ten feet away. He got to his feet and ran towards the horses.

He scrabbled at the straps of his palomino's saddle-bag, before grabbing his gun belt, his Colt still in its holster. Buckling on the belt, he pulled out his sidearm, feeling by its weight that it was still loaded. He swung round and stepped slowly to the rear of the shanty. The three men were out of view but he could hear them talking of where they planned to head for when Hendrix paid them off.

Carlsen cocked his sidearm. Then he stepped away from the shelter of the shanty. One of the men must have seen the movement in the corner of his eye. He let out a warning cry but he was too late. Carlsen fired three times. Each man died instantly, blood and brains spattering over the buffalo grass.

Ethan must have seen him approaching the Bar Circle. As Carlsen reined in at the Big House, Ethan and Jane stepped down to the hard pack, their faces wreathed in smiles.

'Mr Carlsen! Thank the good Lord you're not harmed,' Jane said warmly.

'Sure is good to see you, boss,' Ethan said, grinning broadly.

'Hector assumed you'd been taken to the sheriff and put into jail,' Jane said.

'He had long talks with Mr Morgan and then both of them rode into town.'

'Chet Morgan has said he'll say his piece afore a judge,' said Ethan excitedly.

'Well I'm' – Carlsen broke off with a glance at Jane – 'gosh darned!' he finished. 'When do we reckon Hector will be back?'

'There's Mr Davis now,' Ethan said, pointing over Carlsen's shoulder.

'Jack! Jack!' Davis shouted.

The lawyer spurred on his horse, then bringing the animal to a sudden halt, and jumping to the ground.

'My god! I thought you were dead!'

'I guess I could feel that hemp around my neck,' Carlsen laughed as Davis pumped his outstretched hand. 'I gotta thank you for bringing Morgan 'round.'

'But what about you? What in tarnation happened to you?'

'I'll tell you later. Right now I need to clean up and get some grub.'

Davis appeared quick to realize Carlsen didn't wish to speak in front of Jane Nicholls. He gave a brief nod and turned to Ethan. 'Have Mrs Gittins prepare two meals and bring them over to Mr Carlsen's shanty. Jane, if you'll excuse me, I'll take an early meal with Jack. There's something I need to explain to him.'

Jane nodded. 'Very well, Hector. If I need to know any more, I'm sure you'll tell me.' She looked at the three. 'I'm so pleased we're all here again and safe.'

'I owe it to Ethan that I got back,' Carlsen said. He punched the young man lightly on his arm. 'I'll tell you about it after you've seen to my horse.'

CHAPTER FOURTEEN

When Carlsen walked into the barn the following morning to greet Ethan and take a look at the horses, Hector Davis was hard at work stacking bales of hay. The change from the pasty-faced city dweller to Davis's well-muscled figure surprised even Carlsen. Although Davis may have adopted habits he'd learned out west, the lawyer hadn't lost his respect for the rule of law.

When Carlsen had told him of the shooting of the three men, Davis had been visibly shaken.

'Couldn't you have disarmed them,' he'd asked, 'maybe taken them into Jensen?' It was an instinctive reaction, and then he'd paused for a second, not giving Carlsen the chance to reply. 'No, that's damned foolish! They'd have killed you, whatever Hendrix had ordered.'

Now Davis came striding down the barn. 'Jack, something I forgot to mention last night. Fenner said that the circuit judge could be some weeks before he arrived in Jensen.'

'So what's Morgan about?'

'Fenner's keeping him in the jailhouse for safety, feeding him good grub and enough whiskey.'

'Seems this damned business will never end.'

Ethan called out from the doorway of the barn. 'Boss, Miss Eliza's comin' this way.' He pointed in the direction of the approaching buckboard as Carlsen reached the doorway.

'Now what could Eliza Parsons want out here so early in the morning?' Davis said, standing close behind the pair. The three of them walked across to the hardpack in front of the Big House as Eliza pulled on her reins, bringing the buckboard to a halt.

'Good morning, Eliza,' Carlsen said, a finger touching the rim of his Stetson. 'Miss Jane will have finished her breakfast now.'

'It's you I need to speak with, Jack, although Miss Jane will be involved, too.'

Carlsen exchanged glances with Davis. 'OK, Eliza, we should go into the house.' He turned to Ethan. 'Take charge of Miss Eliza's rig, Ethan.' He held out his hand to Eliza to assist her stepping down from the buckboard and led her up the steps into the house, followed by Davis.

'I'll go and see Jane,' Davis said. 'Take Miss Eliza into the small parlour.'

A few minutes later, Carlsen got to his feet as Jane, and then Davis, entered the parlour.

'How good to see you, Eliza. Mrs Gittins will bring tea shortly.' She smiled. 'A pleasant change from all this coffee I've been drinking.' She took her seat and the two men sat down. 'Now Eliza, what can I do for you?'

'It's really Jack I must speak with but I know this will concern you, too.'

'Go ahead, Miss Eliza,' Davis prompted.

Eliza looked around at them all before replying. 'Sheriff Fenner was killed last night,' she said, her voice low.

'Why? How?' Davis stammered.

'Nobody knows. Nothing was seen. The young deputy

140

found him this morning on the floor of his office.'

'Grant Hendrix,' Carlsen said flatly. 'Did he kill Morgan?'

'Mr Morgan wasn't in the jailhouse. Sheriff Fenner had moved him earlier in the day.'

Carlsen blew out air in a silent whistle. 'So where is he now?'

Eliza looked him straight in the eye. 'In the little shanty, back o' my house.'

Carlsen's jaw dropped. '*What?*'

'Miss Eliza was in Fenner's office, Jack, when I rode in with Morgan. She was asking about you,' Davis said.

'Mr Fenner could see the danger of keeping Mr Morgan in the jailhouse,' Eliza said. Her shoulders lifted a fraction. 'I offered to help.'

'You must stay here, Eliza, until all this is settled,' Jane said briskly.

'Thank you but I don't—'

'Eliza,' Carlsen cut in. 'Please.'

'But—'

'Please.'

Eliza looked away from Carlsen. 'Thank you, Miss Jane, I accept gladly.' Again she looked at all three. 'But there's more,' she said.

'Even more?' Jane said lightly, but seeing the expression on Eliza's face she became serious. 'Please continue.'

'Mayor Castrie wishes to know if Jack will be the sheriff of Jensen until the councilmen can choose another.'

Had a fire-arrow from an Apache Indian been shot into the small parlour, the reaction to Eliza's words could hardly have been greater. Davis jumped up from his chair.

'This is absolute madness! Jack's place is here looking after the Bar Circle. He's played his part. Two days ago he was almost killed. If Grant Hendrix did attack the jailhouse, and I'm betting he did, he'll try again to kill Morgan. Castrie is asking for Jack to gamble with his life. Jensen needs to look after its own affairs.' His face puce with anger, he threw himself into his chair, glaring across the room. 'Surely you agree with me, Jane?'

'Eliza, why does Mayor Castrie think Mr Carlsen can be sheriff, and why hasn't he come here himself?'

'Miss Jane, before Jack took to ranching he had a reputation for—?'

'Enough, Eliza,' Carlsen interrupted softly.

Eliza nodded, pausing for a moment. 'Mayor Castrie thought I would be more successful in persuading Jack to wear the badge.' Her face turned pink and she looked away from the three others.

'Then he was mistaken,' Davis said. 'Jack's duty is to his employer. It could be weeks before the judge visits Jensen.'

'If Mr Carlsen is prepared to be sheriff, a week or two perhaps would have been acceptable,' Jane said. 'But there are important matters regarding the ranch to be dealt with before I go back east and I need him here.'

The four looked around at each other, each struggling to find an answer. Finally Carlsen spoke. 'I've an idea how we can avoid stretchin' this out,' he said. 'I'm not sure if it will work but see what you think.'

With the others in the parlour listening intently, he outlined his plan. When he'd finished talking the three others looked at each other, nodding slowly.

'It could work,' Jane said. 'It's dangerous but if it works, Mr Carlsen will be back with us before long.'

'But what if it doesn't work?' Davis said. 'I'm trying not to be heartless, Jack, but we'll still have a ranch to run even without you around.'

Carlsen's mouth twitched. 'Then you call in Pete Maxton.' He turned to Eliza. 'When this is finished—'

'After this is finished, Jack Carlsen,' Eliza said sharply, 'I do not wish to be standing by your graveside.'

Carlsen stepped down from his saddle, hitched his palomino to the rail and walked along the alley to Eliza's clapboard. Had Morgan been scared off with the death of Sheriff Fenner? He would probably know now that Grant Hendrix would stop at nothing to prevent him appearing before a judge and telling what he'd seen. Hendrix could still manoeuvre to achieve what he was after, Carlsen realized, the Bar Circle in trouble and ripe for easy picking. He skirted Eliza's clapboard and approached the shanty.

'Chet Morgan! You in there?' Carlsen called.

'Jesus Christ!'

Splinters flew from the door of the shanty and a slug caught the rim of his Stetson, sending it flying behind him. He threw himself to the ground, grabbing at the Colt on his belt. For a few seconds nothing moved, and then breathing heavily, he raised his head. Was Hendrix in the shanty? Had Hendrix already found where Morgan was trying to hide and killed him? Carlsen closed his eyes for a moment, thanking Jane for keeping Eliza at the Bar Circle.

'You in the shanty,' he shouted. 'I'm gonna burn you out if you shoot agin.'

There was silence for a few moments. Then from inside the shanty came an answering shout. 'Is that you, Mr Carlsen?'

'Yeah, you crazy bastard! You almost killed me!'

Carlsen got to his feet as the door opened slowly, and a white-faced Morgan peered from the doorway. 'I'm real sorry, Mr Carlsen. I didn't know your voice, an' thought you were Grant Hendrix comin' after me.' He frowned, looking at Carlsen's chest. 'Why you wearin' that badge, Mr Carlsen?'

143

So Morgan hadn't heard about Fenner's death. 'I'll tell you when we get to the jailhouse. Right now we're gonna walk down Main Street so all the townsfolk get a good look at you goin' in the jailhouse with me.'

Morgan took a step back. 'I ain't gonna do no such thing! Grant Hendrix will know where to find me inside a coupla hours.'

'He will, an' he'll try an' get to you,' Carlsen agreed. 'That's when we get hold of him an' then you'll be safe.'

'I ain't gonna do it!'

'You gonna spend the rest of your life in this shanty?'

Morgan shook his head. 'No, I cain't do that.'

'Then walk with me to the jailhouse. If you ain't up to walkin' you can ride my palomino.'

Morgan hesitated for a moment. 'OK, Mr Carlsen, I'll go with you.' He glanced again at the sheriff's badge pinned to Carlsen's shirt. 'An' you can tell me what's goin' on.'

The young deputy stood in front of the desk, waiting for further orders from the new sheriff. Carlsen, his arms resting on the desk, toyed with his pen, wondering what local influence had enabled this young man to put on a deputy's badge.

'OK, is that clear? You take water and grub, an' you ride out a mile from town in the direction of the Lazy Y. You see a bunch of riders coming this way, you hightail it back here. You stay there until mid-afternoon. You got that?'

The young man nodded vigorously. 'Yes, sir.'

'Back here you clear Main Street of all citizens. I don't want innocent townsfolk caught in a gunfight.'

Before he could say anything further, the door from the street opened. Carlsen didn't take his eyes off the deputy.

'Hold on there,' he addressed the newcomer. 'I'm busy now.'

'From what I hear you're gonna be a damn sight busier.'

Carlsen head snapped around. 'Hank Mather! You're s'posed to be in Cheyenne. Get some coffee while I finish here.' He turned to the deputy again. 'After makin' sure all the townsfolk know what's goin' on, you get home.'

'But I gotta stand with you, Mr Carlsen. I'm your deputy,' the young man protested.

Yes, and you're too young to die in the Main Street of a Wyoming trading town, Carlsen thought. He'd planned to make that clear to the young man. But now he had a chance to save the young man's pride.

'Yeah, I was expectin' you would. But Mr Mather's here now, and we work better just the two of us together.'

'The sheriff's right, kid,' Mather said, bringing his coffee across from the pot-bellied stove. 'You're gonna be more use to us keeping lookout and clearin' the street.'

'OK, go get your horse,' Carlsen said, 'an' remember your slicker cos it's probably gonna rain.'

'Right away, Sheriff!'

The deputy turned and strode from the office like a man preparing for battle.

Mather's mouth puckered. 'He gotta pa with influence?'

Carlsen grinned. 'I guess so.'

'An' what the hell's that pinned to your chest? I thought you was in the cattle business.'

'It ain't fer long. Anyways, you're s'posed to be in a saloon in Cheyenne, a scatter-gun 'cross your knees.'

Mather shrugged. 'I reached the second stage station, gotta bunk fer the night, an' got to thinkin' 'bout what you said. Times changin' an' all that. Then I heard folks talkin' about troubles here.' He glanced towards the window overlooking Main Street for a moment. 'Hell, my pa ran a dry goods store. Without the War I guess I'd have followed him. With that money Mr Davis paid me, I reckon I can set up in

145

Jensen.' He took a gulp of his coffee. 'So what barrel o' tar you got yourself into?'

Carlsen took a couple of minutes explaining the events of the previous few days. When Mather had nodded his understanding Carlsen added, 'I'm damned glad you're here, Hank.'

'How many we up against?'

'Seven mebbe. Grant Hendrix himself an' half a dozen.'

Mather frowned. 'How many we got?'

Carlsen's mouth twitched. 'Me an' you.'

Mather leaned back in his chair, blowing a silent whistle. 'No Volunteers?'

'They left this mornin', parading fer Governor Thayer in Cheyenne. There's family men left in town who couldn't hit a barn door from five yards.'

Mather breathed in deeply. 'We come outta this I'm gonna be a good citizen, go to church on Sunday, help at harvest dinners.'

Carlsen grinned. 'Fine, Hank. Meanwhile, you walk along to the General Store and buy up as much Winchester and Colt ammo as you can carry. Tell the German who runs the store Mayor Castrie has said the town will pay.'

CHAPTER FIFTEEN

The door of the sheriff's office burst open and Carlsen's young deputy rushed through the doorway spraying rainwater across the office, raindrops dripping from the brim of his Stetson.

'They're comin', Mr Carlsen! They're on their way,' he said breathlessly.

'You sure it's Hendrix?'

'I'm sure. I did as you said an' took a long look at 'em through my spyglass.'

'An' you saw Hendrix's red reins?'

'Yeah, I did, Mr Carlsen. He's ridin' in the middle of a line. Three riders either side.'

Carlsen's expression hardened. 'OK, make sure you clear the street. Lots of folks will have stayed at home outta the rain, but you tell anyone you see there's gonna be gunfightin' soon.'

'Sheriff?'

Carlsen knew what he intended to say, and thought well of him for it, but he'd made his decision. 'Once the street is clear you get home. That's an order!'

The deputy nodded reluctantly. 'Sure thing, Mr Carlsen.'

Alone, Carlsen got to his feet, crossed the office, and took down the Winchester long gun, which rested on the pegs pinned to the stucco wall. He shoved two boxes of slugs into his pockets, took a deep breath, and went out to the boardwalk. Across Main Street on the roof of the General Store, Mather, half-crouched, was partly shielded by a metal pipe. He raised a hand to show he knew Hendrix and his no-goods were on their way.

The regular beat of horses' hoofs reached Carlsen. Moments later, he saw the line of riders reach the start of Main Street, red reins on the centre horse. The rancher meant to attack the jailhouse, he must know that Morgan was inside after being paraded along Main Street earlier in the day. The line of riders slowed as the men advanced down Main Street. Seven men, wearing slickers against the rain, their hats pulled low, and all with long guns resting against the pommels of their saddles. Carlsen stepped down to Main Street, partly shielded by a water trough. He leaned his Winchester against the trough and cupped his hands around his mouth.

'Hendrix!' he shouted. 'You come any closer to the jail-house and men are gonna be killed!'

The line of riders kept advancing down the street.

'Hendrix,' Carlsen shouted again. 'I got ten men around you. Your men are gonna die if you come closer to the jail-house.'

Above the sounds of the rain beating down, he heard the word 'Volunteers' and hoots and whistles from the line of riders. He bent down and grabbed his Winchester, then raised his hand, clutching a square of red cloth.

There was the sound of a shot, the levering of a Winchester, followed immediately by another shot. Two men fell from their saddles and the line broke. Shouted warnings rang out as the remaining five riders pulled around the heads of their horses. At that moment a buggy, its driver protected from the rain by a black rain-hood, turned into Main Street from the alley leading to the livery. Carlsen saw immediately there was no chance he or Mather could risk a shot without the chance of hitting the driver.

Carlsen swore. 'Goddamn that deputy!'

But in that same moment he knew. Hendrix! A single shot was fired by the driver of the carriage. Above the beating rain sounded an anguished cry from Mather. Carlsen saw his partner slump to the roof of the store. A moment later, a long gun bounced down the front of the store and fell into the street.

Carlsen threw himself from the boardwalk to take cover behind the water trough. As he did so, he saw the carriage swing away as its horse was hauled around. Then water sprayed from the trough to mix with the rain and shots from a sidearm sounded along the street. Risking a look above the edge of the trough, Carlsen saw Hendrix leap from the carriage and reach the boardwalk opposite the jailhouse before he was lost in the shadows.

Carlsen took a deep breath and pushed himself to a crouch, scrubbing away soft wet dirt from his hands on his pants. He had a choice. Either remain where he was and wait for Hendrix to make a move. Or maybe he could catch him unawares by crossing the street. Carlsen peered around the trough to where he thought Hendrix was likely to be. Main Street, which he'd always thought too narrow for a town of Jensen's size, suddenly appeared much wider. Could he get across before Hendrix cut him down?

'One way to find out,' he muttered aloud.

He put a hand on the edge of the trough and pulled himself up, trying to keep the top half of his body low down. He thumbed back the hammer of his Colt. A couple of shots would maybe keep Hendrix's head down. He filled his lungs with air, anchored his boots in the soft ground to get a good start and flung himself forward to run across the street, zigzagging and pulling the trigger of his Colt as he ran. Shots rang out from the shadows and slugs cut the air around him as his lungs filled to bursting before he threw himself up the steps to the boardwalk, scrabbling across the timbers to reach the cover of a water barrel.

'I'm gettin' too old for this malarkey,' he muttered aloud.

He took off his Stetson and peered above the barrel.

'Hendrix!' he shouted. 'You got what you wanted! It's between you and me now.'

Splinters flew from the top of the barrel as Hendrix fired twice, the chips of wood stinging the side of Carlsen's face. He ducked down, feeling the trickle of blood from the lobe of his ear.

'An' we ain't shootin' at targets now, Carlsen!' Hendrix shouted. 'I'm gonna kill you an' then I'm gonna kill that lyin' sonovabitch Morgan.'

It was Hendrix's first mistake. Carlsen judged the rancher to be standing in the doorway of the General Store; he had heard the faint ring of the bell which hung by the doorway of the store. They both knew where the other had taken shelter. Carlsen's mind raced. A charge down the boardwalk would get him killed. Hendrix would see him coming and pick him off.

But the same for Hendrix, he realized. Neither of them could risk stepping out from where they were taking shelter. His mind churned. Maybe the barrel was the answer. He reached down and turned the faucet. Water gushed out across the boards and drained into the street. He fired one shot in the direction of the store to keep Hendrix from running, and then reloaded his Colt ready for what he knew was ahead.

Finally, no more water ran from the faucet. Gripping the heavy barrel by its rim, and taking care to remain shielded,

Carlsen turned the barrel on to its side. Half-bent, he gave the barrel a shove, his outstretched arm holding his Colt atop the barrel side. The barrel didn't move and he pushed hard with his shoulder. Slowly, the barrel began to move, gathering pace as it rolled down the slight incline of the boards.

Five yards on he could see the doorway of the store. Slugs smashed harmlessly into the sides of the barrel as Hendrix must have realized what Carlsen was about. Carlsen fired twice. Then clearly through the still air, following the rain, Carlsen heard the metallic clicks of a trigger being pulled on an empty sidearm, quickly followed by the clattering of boots on the boards as the rancher ran from the doorway of the store. Carlsen jumped up in time to see Hendrix turning the corner into an alley which Carlsen knew led to a line of clapboards.

Was Hendrix going for his horse? He'd come into town by the buckboard and probably thought he'd leave in it. Carlsen ran down the alley, keeping close to the timbers of the dry goods store for protection. As he reached the end of the alley, he heard the sounds of wood being smashed and seconds later, a woman screamed. What the hell was going on?

He reached the end of the store and peered around. The door of the second clapboard had been kicked open, splinters of wood lying on the ground. Carlsen knew then what Hendrix was planning and felt as if he'd been punched in the stomach.

Hendrix must have known that Carlsen was close by.

'Carlsen! I've the Widow Brown and her five brats in here. You're gonna get me a horse and lemme ride outta town.'

'An' if I don't?'

'I'll kill the woman an' her brats. An' then it's still you an' me.'

151

Carlsen felt a claw rip at his heart. It was Green Valley all over again. Was this the way his life was to change once more? If Hendrix rode out of town, he'd be fleeing from everything at the Lazy Y. So why not let Hendrix run? Jane Nicholls and the Bar Circle demanded his loyalty, not the law. Yet Fenner had died defending the law. Hector Davis would think less of him if he let Hendrix avoid facing a judge. He swallowed a couple of times, making sure his voice was strong.

'You hear me, Hendrix?'

'I hear you.'

'I'll get you a horse. You let Widow Brown free.'

'First you bring the horse, an' make damned sure you bring a strong one.'

Carlsen dropped his Colt into its holster. 'I'm on my way.'

He turned on his heel and strode quickly along the alley-way and along the boards, skirting the barrel and picking up his hat before turning in the alleyway leading to the livery. There was sweat on his forehead, and he guessed he was white-faced. His stomach heaved with the choice before him. He remembered Widow Brown from the town's annual shindig the previous year. Lots of townsfolk had crowded around the shooting match between himself and Grant Hendrix. As he'd walked to take up his shooting position, she'd given him a wide smile and wished him luck. He'd heard that one of the Volunteers was courting her. Zeke Gale, the liveryman, came rushing towards him.

'What the hell's happening out there, Jack?'

'I need a strong horse, Zeke.' Quickly, he explained the situation.

'Fer chris'sakes!' Gale turned on his heel. 'Here, take mine. It's already saddled.'

'Thanks. I'll see you get paid.'

'I've had coffee with Emily Brown a coupla times. You

152

save her. That's all the payment I need.'

Carlsen frowned. 'Those shutters she's got. They open in or out?'

'In,' Gale said promptly. 'When they're closed they've a coupla fancy pictures on the inside.'

Carlsen nodded. 'OK.' He breathed in deeply, turning the horse's head to lead the animal out of the livery and along Main Street. Shadows were growing longer when he reached the alleyway leading to the clapboard of Widow Brown. He reached the low picket fence of the house and stopped.

'I got the horse, Hendrix!'

Did a shutter move an inch?

'Toss your Colt over the fence and back off.'

Carlsen dropped the reins of the horse, pulled out his Colt and tossed it over the fence. Then he backed away, not taking his eyes off the shutter.

'I'm comin' out!' The tone of Hendrix's voice had gone up a notch. 'No shootin', I give you my word.'

Hendrix's word wasn't worth a pennyworth of cow dung, Carlsen thought, shifting his feet, and keeping his eyes on the shutter. He saw it move an inch.

With an explosion of energy he leapt forward, cleared the picket fence and threw himself at the shutter, tearing it from its hinges and sending it flying before him across the room, the screams of the woman and her children rending the air. Carlsen rolled on to his back. For a split second the two men stared across the room at each other. Then Carlsen shot Hendrix twice in the head with his pocket pistol, the blue stone in the butt pressing against the flesh of his thumb.

CHAPTER SIXTEEN

'All your boxes are on the wagon, Miss Jane. Two rooms are reserved for you and Hector at the hotel in town. This will give you chance to rest before boarding the UP to Cheyenne.'

'Thank you, Mr Carlsen. Will you be driving the surrey to Jensen?'

'No, ma'am. Ethan was all fired-up for that honour. I'll be riding along with you on my palomino.'

Jane smiled. 'Just as it was at the beginning of summer.'

'Almost, ma'am. But Sean was drivin' you that day.'

'You will make sure Sean is well taken care of?'

'Don't you worry, Miss Jane. When you come back next spring, Sean'll be here as good as he ever was.'

They both turned from where they were standing in front of the Big House as Hector Davis – wearing a city suit and carrying a derby hat – came through the doorway.

'How smart you look, Hector,' exclaimed Jane.

Davis ran a finger inside his stiff collar. 'Why in tarnation we men wear these collars, I'll never know. I only wish I was in range clothes.'

'Mebbe you can set a new style in New York, Hector.'

Davis smiled. 'I don't think so, Jack.' He looked towards the surrey as Ethan brought the carriage across the hard-pack from the barn. 'All arranged in Jensen, Jack?'

Carlsen nodded. 'All fixed.'

Mrs Gittins and Lucy appeared in the doorway behind them. A tear glistened on the housekeeper's cheek. 'Goodbye, Miss Jane. I hope after you're married, you'll bring your husband to see us.'

'I shall be lucky if President Hayes allows him to leave Washington, but I shall do my best to persuade him. Goodbye, Lucy, I know you have both worked hard this summer. Thank you.'

Ethan brought the surrey to a halt as Jane, her maid, and Hector stepped up to it. Carlsen slipped the palomino's reins from the rail and mounted to guide the horse alongside them.

Carlsen was chatting with the hotel clerk when Hector Davis came down the stairs. His city suit had been discarded and he now wore the greenhorn's clothing he'd worn on his first arrival in Jensen Flats. In his hand, he carried the huge Californian spurs he'd previously exchanged at the General Store.

'Tom Rudman wants those back,' Carlsen reminded him.

'With pleasure,' Hector said. 'No decent cowboy would wear them. JB's resting for an hour so we're in the clear.'

Carlsen smiled broadly. 'Care for a beer, Mr Davis?'

Hector's grin was equally broad. 'A splendid idea, Mr Carlsen.'

He held up a hat decorated with bright coins.

'I'll carry this to the Dollar,' he said. 'Friends of mine in town would throw rocks at me if they saw me wearing it.'

Outside the Silver Dollar, Carlsen settled himself on one of the chairs on the boardwalk overlooking Main Street. His legs were outstretched and he had tipped his Stetson a couple of inches lower over his nose while he surveyed the town. A couple of minutes later, Hector Davis walked a horse, borrowed for the occasion from the livery, along Main Street to the rail in front of the saloon. As he wound his mount's reins around the rail, Carlsen raised a lazy hand. It was a signal Davis was looking for. The no-good Will was in the saloon, playing cards.

Davis walked up the five steps and pushed through the batwing doors.

Carlsen breathed in; the next few minutes would show if what he'd promised the New York lawyer would come to pass. If it all went wrong, he'd have to be ready to enter the saloon and save Hector from a beating. Will would have bad memories from their last encounter and he'd be keen not to lose face in front of his fellow card-players.

Suddenly, there was a loud clatter from inside the Dollar as if a table had been overturned. There were loud shouts and then the sound of heavy footsteps across the boards. The batwing door of the saloon swung open and a figure staggered past Carlsen, missed his footing on the top step and went crashing on to his face on to the hardpack before rolling over to look at Carlsen, a red mark on his cheekbone.

'That's gonna be a big bruise afore nightfall,' Carlsen said evenly.

'It took two of them to throw me out,' said Hector Davis, scrambling to his feet. 'You ready for that beer?'

Carlsen grinned. 'Sure am, Hector.'

They stepped into the saloon. Close to the tables, two men were dragging across the boards the unconscious figure of Will. They dropped Will's hands and held up their own.

'No trouble, Mr Carlsen,' the taller of the two said. 'Will shot his mouth off and couldn't back it with his fists.'

'Mr Davis, Jack, drinks on the house.' Josh, behind the bar, put two glasses in front of the men. He looked at Davis. 'Seems you come some way this summer, Mr Davis.'

*

As Carlsen watched, the ranch-hand Fred Baker rolled the wagon to where he would load the boxes being taken back east by Jane Nicholls and Hector Davis. The Bar Circle surrey drew up alongside the UP train as steam blew from the smoke-stack of the engine. A few feet away, a door opened and a blue-uniformed conductor stepped from the car to place in position a small flight of steps. Carlsen held out a hand to assist Jane Nicholls to alight from the surrey while Davis and the maid stepped to the ground on the other side.

'Thank you, Ethan,' Jane said, as the young man's face turned crimson with pleasure.

She turned to Carlsen. 'It has been a wonderful summer.' She paused for a second before adding, 'Maybe a little too exciting on occasion.' She looked directly at him. 'I know the Bar Circle will be in good hands until I return. When the lawyers have done their work, we shall add the Lazy Y to our spread.'

'We all look forward to you comin' back, Miss Jane. The men are already askin' when you'll ride out with 'em agin.'

'Then I mustn't disappoint them.' She smiled up at him. 'And next year we'll attend the town's spring dance.'

'Then I hope you'll save me a waltz an' a two-step, Miss Jane.'

Her eyes sparkled and a smile curved her lips.

'Honestly, Mr Carlsen, you are incorrigible!'

He didn't know what that word meant but her smile was warm so he guessed it was fine. For a brief moment her gloved hand rested on his arm. Then she turned and stepped up into the train.

'Goodbye, Jack.' Davis shook his hand. 'Next year you can teach me to shoot a Colt!'

'That's a promise, Hector. You jest make sure you come back with Miss Jane.'

Five minutes later, with an ear-blasting discharge of steam, the wheels of the UP locomotive began to slowly turn and within a few seconds, the last of the railcars passed Carlsen and he stood there, looking along the tracks until the train disappeared around the bend. Carlsen turned to the surrey.

'OK, Ethan, back to the ranch. I'll be in town for a few hours but I'll be back afore dark.'

'Right you are, Mr Carlsen. The stage came in when we were drivin' through town. We got anythin' we need to pick up?'

'No, you jest go back to the ranch.'

Ethan raised his hand in acknowledgement and turned the head of the pony, leaving the railroad tracks behind him. Carlsen stood for a few seconds, gazing towards the bend where the UP had vanished from sight, although if he strained his ears he could just hear the sounds of the engine as it headed towards Cheyenne.

In the short space of a few weeks of summer, his life had changed once again. Sure, he'd had to take out his Colt but it was for the last time, save for the annual shooting contest. But he'd be shooting only at wooden targets. There'd be no more shooting at his fellow human beings. He hadn't wanted to kill Grant Hendrix or any of those no-goods Hendrix had hired. If Hendrix hadn't tried to have him hanged for the killing of his father, they could maybe have worked something out. His mouth twisted. Or then again, maybe not.

Anyway, from now on he would be thinking only of the land he was responsible for and the cattle which made it possible for men, yes, and women, to make an honest and decent living. But first, there were a couple of things he needed to look into.

'How's it goin' with the councilmen?' Carlsen asked the hotel clerk.

'They've been in there since the stage arrived,' the clerk said. 'Reckon they should be finished about now.'

'OK, I'll take a seat an' wait.'

'I'll have some coffee brought if you wish.'

Carlsen shook his head. 'I'm fine, thanks.'

He took a seat on the red plush chair a few feet from the street door of the hotel and settled down. He hadn't long to wait. A sudden noise of voices at the end of the corridor indicated that the council meeting was over. Ahead of the group was Hank Mather, a shirt sleeve bulging from the pad covering the bullet wound where Hendrix had winged him. A broad grin of triumph was on his face. He saw Carlsen and strode across to him as Carlsen got to his feet.

'I've got it, Jack, I've got it!'

'They've made a fine choice,' Carlsen said, pumping his old partner's hand in undisguised pleasure. 'When do you take over?'

'Straightaways. I'm gonna take the oath today and then I put on the badge!' Mather almost did a little jig. 'Sheriff of Jensen Flats! Life sure is damned strange.'

'Get yourself set an' we'll have a beer to celebrate. Mebbe we'll break a rule an' have a whiskey.'

'Sure thing, Jack. An' thanks agin, partner.'

'You got the job, Hank. It was down to you.'

After leaving the hotel, Carlsen walked along the boards until he'd passed the General Store and stepped down to the hard pack of the alley, which led to the line of neat clapboards at the rear of the Main Street stores. He hesitated for a moment, remembering which one he wanted. His thoughts jumped to the moment when Morgan had almost killed him. He brushed them aside. Morgan was now working at the Bar Circle, no longer needing to say his piece in front of the judge.

He pushed open the gate and walked up to the door and knocked. A young girl, hardly out of school, opened the door.

Carlsen took off his hat. 'I'm callin' on Mrs Parsons,' he said.

Eliza Parsons appeared behind the girl. 'It's all right, Millie. Mr Carlsen and I will go into the parlour.'

Carlsen bent and unstrapped his spurs, and then followed Eliza along the short passage to the parlour.

'Sit down, Jack, what brings you here?'

Carlsen coughed, clearing his throat. 'Eliza, I want to ask a favour of you.'

Eliza raised her eyebrows. 'And what would that be?'

'Well, when you go to Cheyenne in the winter, do you ever dance the waltz and the two-step?'

With an amused smile on her lips, Eliza nodded. 'Yes, I do.'

Carlsen breathed in deeply. 'Then, Eliza, would you teach me them dances?'

Eliza pressed her lips together as if resisting the temptation to laugh. 'I can do that, Jack. But you have to do something for me.'

'Sure, Eliza, you name it.'

'You'll accompany me to church on Sunday.'

He wasn't expecting that. But the more he thought about it, the more he liked the idea.

'I can do that,' he said. 'But people will think . . .' His voice trailed away.

'Yes, maybe.'

They exchanged smiles. Then Carlsen held out his hand to her.

'Then I reckon they'd be thinkin' jest right, Eliza.'